Rendezvous with Death

Jessica opened her purse, took out a flash-light and walked toward the warehouse. Outside the entrance she stopped and took a deep breath. Then she went inside.

It was totally dark. She shivered, licked her lips and called out: "Hello?"

The silence was total. Then she heard a sound. Footsteps? Something being dragged? Fighting down a rising panic, Jessica called out again: "Who's there?"

She shone her flashlight and nearly screamed out loud as the beam lighted on a human figure.

It was a woman, and she was staggering toward Jessica, dragging her feet. Her face was ashen, her expression ghastly. She seemed to be wearing a dress with a garish pattern of scarlet patches.

Then Jessica saw that the scarlet was blood ...

MURDER, SHE WROTE

#3

LOVERS AND OTHER KILLERS
A NOVEL BY JAMES ANDERSON

Based on the Universal television series
"Murder, She Wrote"

Created by Peter S. Fischer and Richard Levinson &
William Link
Adapted from the episodes
"Lovers and Other Killers,"
Written by Peter S. Fischer
and "It's a Dog's Life,"
Written by Mark Giles and Linda Shank

AVON
PUBLISHERS OF BARD, CAMELOT, DISCUS AND FLARE BOOKS

MURDER, SHE WROTE #3: LOVERS AND OTHER KILLERS
is an original publication of Avon Books. This work has never
before appeared in book form. This work is a novel. Any similarity
to actual persons or events is purely coincidental.

AVON BOOKS
A division of
The Hearst Corporation
1790 Broadway
New York, New York 10019

Copyright © 1986 by MCA Publishing Rights, a Division of MCA Inc.
Published by arrangement with MCA Publishing Rights, a Division
of MCA Inc.
Library of Congress Catalog Card Number: 85-90395
ISBN: 0-380-89938-8

First Avon Printing, February 1986

AVON TRADEMARK REG. U. S. PAT. OFF. AND IN
OTHER COUNTRIES, MARCA REGISTRADA, HECHO EN
U.S.A.

Printed in the U.S.A.

WFH   10   9   8   7   6   5   4   3   2   1

Prologue

"**B**UT, Inspector, we know Haskell was shot in the temple. The bullet exited at the base of the skull. A *downward* trajectory. Nell Foster was in a wheelchair. Haskell would have had to be on his knees for her to have shot him from a sitting position."

The Inspector smiled grimly. "Well, why not?"

"*Why not?*" The Sergeant stared. "You saying he got on his knees, begging her not to—"

The Inspector shook his head and drew on his pipe. "Not at all. But he was blackmailing her, right? This was a payoff. Or so he thought. She has the money in an envelope. But instead of handing it to him, she hurls it contemptuously on the floor at his feet. He bends to pick it up—and at that moment she brings the pistol from under the rug on her knees and shoots him."

The Sergeant stared. "But that's brilliant, Inspector—"

Jessica Fletcher stopped writing. Oops! She couldn't have the Sergeant staring again already. She thought for a moment, and changed the second *stared* to *whistled*.

Then she read the page over. She crossed out *grimly* after *smiled*. That was a cliché. People were always smiling grimly in novels. Yet she couldn't ever remember seeing anyone do it in real life. Apart from that, the page seemed okay.

Though, was the Inspector being all that brilliant? Was the point, on the contrary, just a little elementary?

Jessica sighed. It was so difficult to tell what would fool

mystery buffs and what wouldn't. Sometimes what you considered your cleverest twists passed unnoticed, while points that seemed to you quite ordinary were picked out as being especially ingenious.

At that moment there came a sharp and familiar rat-tat on the back door. With relief—anything to stop work for a few minutes—she called: "Come in, Ethan."

The door opened, and Ethan Cragg entered the room. He was a tough-looking, weather-beaten man in his mid-fifties who had been a friend of her late husband Frank, and who, since Frank's death, had been a good friend to his widow.

Now he grinned. "Somehow, I thought I'd find you working at the kitchen table as usual, Jess. What happened to that smart writing room you were going to get fixed up?"

Jessica looked around the kitchen. "Oh, I don't know. I've certainly got plenty of spare rooms, but somehow I work so well in here. Perhaps because, before I started writing, the only creative work I ever did was done at that stove."

He nodded at the pile of typewritten papers on the table. "New story coming along all right, is it?"

She shrugged. "Well, I am getting there—slowly. Somehow, though, I don't think it's much good."

"At least that's an improvement on your other books. In the past, you've been quite *sure* they're no good—until they've been published and sold millions."

"Oh, don't exaggerate, Ethan. My books don't sell in *millions*."

"They do pretty well, though, don't they?"

"I suppose you could say that."

"You're a best-selling author."

She pursed her lips. "I just about qualify."

"And those critic guys like you."

"Most of them seem to."

"So of course this book's good. Quit worrying."

She smiled. "You're a great comfort, Ethan. Somehow, though, I can't help worrying."

He eyed her closely. "You don't look well, Jess. Reckon you've been working too hard. You need a rest."

"Some hope."

"Listen: you've published three books on the trot, you're working on a fourth—and the only breaks you've had you've spent solving real-life murders."

She nodded thoughtfully. "Life has been a bit hectic, I agree. But I wanted to capitalize on the success of *The Corpse Danced at Midnight* while it was still fresh in people's minds."

"Okay, but now you're established. You're not short of cash. So why not take a vacation?"

"I have to finish this book. I've got a deadline."

"Then right after you've finished it."

"There'll be so many other things to do."

"Tell me, when did you last take one—a real one?"

"Oh, I don't remember exactly. It was with Frank."

"There you are, then. That's too long. So how about it?"

"I'm not good at doing nothing, Ethan. But . . . well, I'll think about it."

He raised his arms in despair. "I give up. I've done my best."

As his arms rose she noticed that he was holding a bundle of letters in one hand.

"What are those?" she asked, pointing.

"Oh, sorry—nearly forgot. They're yours. I met the mailman at your gate."

He handed the letters to her.

"Thank you."

She started shuffling through them, discarding the bills and the obvious junk mail. She was left with two letters, both addressed in hands that looked familiar but which for the moment she couldn't place.

She held them at arm's length, one in each hand, and gazed at them.

"Now, who are these from?"

"Why not open them and find out?"

3

"Ethan, one of the chief pleasures of getting letters is not opening them—trying to guess who they're from."

"Strange letters worry me till they're open: I always expect it to be bad news."

"You're a natural-born pessimist. And you tell *me* not to worry."

She peered at the slightly blurred postmark on the letter in her right hand. "Seattle, Washington. Oh, of course, it's from Edmund."

"Edmund."

"Edmund Gerard. You remember: an old friend of mine, Gwen Gerard, died a few months back?"

"Oh, yeah—you were upset at having to miss her funeral, I remember."

"Yes, it was unavoidable. Edmund was her husband. He's dean of students at Sequoia University. I wonder what he can be writing to me about."

As he opened his mouth, she raised her hand to forestall his comments. "All in good time, Ethan."

Then she squinted at the postmark on the other letter.

"Kentucky. Can't read the town. I don't think I know anyone in Kentucky." She held the letter out for him to see. "A woman's writing, this one, wouldn't you say?"

Ethan laughed. "I wouldn't know, Jess. Anyway, I got to be going."

"Oh, wait and see who this one is from now. You've earned that."

Quickly she ripped open the envelope and drew out the letter. She glanced at the first page, frowned, turned to the back and looked at the signature. Then her face cleared.

"Oh, it's from Abby."

"Well, dang my hide!" Ethan slapped his thigh with the palm of his hand in mock amazement. "Abby! Who'd have thought it?"

Jessica laughed. "Sorry, Ethan. Abigail Freestone, my cousin. She's British."

"What's she doing in Kentucky?"

"That's what I'm trying to find out." She was scanning

4

the letter. "She's at some place called Langley Manor."
Her eyes ran on. "Oh, horses, of course."

"What do you mean?"

"Horses are Abby's life. She was one of the best train-
ers of show jumpers in England. Seems this man—er,
Denton Langley—keeps lots. He's put Abby in charge of
schooling them. My, she'll love that."

"That's fine. Well, I really must be getting along—"

"Hang on, Ethan, this'll please you."

"What's that?"

"She wants me to go and stay with her."

"Great, I hope you go."

"Listen." She read aloud: " 'I have a very cosy little
cottage on the estate, quite close to the big house. I say
little, but there's plenty of room for a guest. I've told the
Langleys about my cousin Jessica, the famous writer, and
they're all longing to meet you. I do hope you'll come.
One small word of warning though: you will be expected
to come hunting.' "

Ethan's brow puckered. "Not much of a hand with a rifle
are you, Jess?"

Jessica smiled. "I think she means fox hunting."

He looked alarmed. "What—on horseback?"

"That is the conventional way, I believe."

"Say, that's dangerous. I don't trust those critters."

"Foxes?"

"No—horses."

"There speaks the true sailor."

"You ever ridden?"

"A little—at one time."

"Well, they say it's something you never forget."

"That I believe to be a myth. However, I suppose I'll
find out."

"You mean you're going?"

"Well, you know, Ethan, I very well might . . . after
I've finished the book. It's a lovely part of the country, I
believe, though I've never been there. And I'm very fond
of Abby. She's a sweet girl—if a trifle dotty. Well, I say

5

girl, because that's what she's always seemed to me, but she must be nearly forty now. I'd like to see her again."

"Then go and enjoy yourself."

"If I can fit it in, I will. Anyway, let's see what Edmund has to say."

She tore open the letter with the Seattle postmark and started to read. After a few seconds she gave a sudden gasp.

"Oh, I couldn't possibly!"

Ethan glanced at her sharply. "Couldn't what?"

"Lecture." She looked up at him, her face a study. "He wants me to lecture—to the students *and* the faculty."

"What about?"

"The crime story."

"Well, why not? You know enough about them, don't you?"

"I'm not at all sure I do." She glanced down at the letter again. "I mean, he suggests three lectures over a week: one on the history of the genre—which means I'd have to go back to Poe, and Wilkie Collins and Conan Doyle; another on the crime story's place in literature; and another on the technique of writing them—how I set about it."

"So what?"

"Well, I'm not at all sure I know how I set about it. I just sit down and think—and then write."

"Then tell 'em that."

"Fine lecture that would make! No, I shall write back and politely decline."

"You won't."

"What do you mean?"

"You're not one to duck a challenge like this, Jess. Besides, you might do your profession a bit of good."

"I don't understand."

"Well, weren't you saying the other day that the highbrow students of literature at the universities don't take the mystery story seriously enough?"

"Yes, I was."

"Well, maybe this is your chance to make some of 'em sit up and take notice."

"Certainly somebody should do that. But I don't think I'm the one to do it. I've had no experience."

"You've been a teacher."

"I've taught high school. There's a big difference between that and a university."

"Principle's the same, I reckon."

"Perhaps . . . up to a point. But aside from that, there's my deadline."

"When's this Edmund fellow want you?"

Jessica consulted the letter again. "He suggests the fifteenth. That's just over two weeks—a week this side of my deadline."

"Can't you speed up—finish the book before then?"

"I doubt it. I'm not good when I try to speed up. I'm a slow, careful, finicky writer. I rewrite a lot. I like to get everything as good as I can make it."

"You're too much of a perfectionist."

"I shall never achieve perfection—but I always aim for it." Jessica sighed. She was looking the picture of misery.

Ethan said, "Well, it's up to you. I'll lay odds now, though, that you will go; and you'll be a hit—just as you'll wow 'em down in Kentucky."

He chuckled suddenly.

"What's the matter?" she asked.

"I was just thinking: for years you didn't leave Cabot Cove. Since you wrote *Corpse* you been to New York City, Los Angeles—and now it's going to be Seattle and Kentucky. Talk about all points of the compass."

"I haven't been yet, Ethan."

"You will, Jess, you will."

He turned for the door. "Well, so long. See you later."

"Bye, Ethan. And thanks for being such a morale-booster."

After he'd left, Jessica returned to the exploits of her brilliant, pipe-puffing Inspector. But she found it difficult to concentrate. What on earth would she say to all those eggheads? And how, after all these years, would she manage on a horse?

7

Chapter One

THE taxi drew up outside the fashionable apartment block. The driver glanced over his shoulder.

"Hey, lady, we're there."

The woman in the back opened her eyes and looked around.

"What?"

"You're home."

"Oh? What time is it?" Her speech was slightly slurred.

He glanced at his watch. "Eleven-thirty." Then, ironically, he added: "P.M."

"What am I doing home as early as this?" She glanced sideways, as if expecting to see somebody. "And why am I on my own?"

"Don't ask me, lady. I only brought you here. You hailed me outside the Ninety-Nine bar, if that's any help. You were alone then."

The woman nodded slowly. "Oh yes, I remember now. I was stood up. Would you believe that, cabbie? Me—Alison Brevard—was stood up." She frowned. "Or should that be *I*? Would you stand me up, cabbie?"

He sighed. "Look, lady, I'm a happily married man. I only been married six months. And I'd like to get home to my wife. Okay?"

"I don't drink normally, you know. But it's a shock to the system, a thing like that. A girl needs a bracer after a thing like that."

"Yeah, sure. Listen, let me give you a hand inside—"

"No, no." She raised her hand in negation. "I can manage. How much?"

"Six-fifty."

"Okay." She fumbled in a small silver evening bag, took out a bill, squinted at it, then passed it to the driver. "How much is that?"

"Twenty bucks." He started to delve in his pocket.

"All right—keep it."

"Gee, thanks."

She eyed him more closely. "Say, you're cute. Come up and have a drink."

"Lady, I explained—"

"I know—you're a mappily harried . . . I mean happily . . . say, that's good: mappily harried. I like that. What they call things like that? Something to do with spoons, isn't it?"

"Listen, Mrs.—Miss—Ms.—"

"Brevard. But you can call me Alison."

"Listen, Alison, why don't you go indoors, go up to your apartment, and go straight to bed? What you need is a good night's sleep."

"You mean go to bed at eleven-thirty?"

"That's right."

"On my own?"

"That's what I'd recommend."

She gave a little giggle. "Well, it would certainly have novelty value. You know, I might very well try out your suggestion, Harry."

"Name's Bill."

"What's that?"

"Skip it." He got out hastily and opened the rear door.

Alison Brevard emerged slowly, staggering a little as her feet touched the sidewalk. Bill caught her by the elbow.

"Thanks, Harry. You're a real gentleman. How much I owe you?"

"You paid me. You going to be all right now?"

"Oh, sure. I live here, you know. You like it?"

"Yeah . . . swell. Well, good night."

"Night, Harry. See you around."

She stood watching him rather wistfully as he climbed back in his cab and drove off.

As the car disappeared down the street, she called out suddenly: "Spoonerism. That's what you call it when you mix your words . . ."

She turned, went slowly through the revolving doors and crossed the lobby to the elevator, swaying ever so slightly as she walked.

Alison Brevard was in her late thirties. She had dyed blond hair, was tall, and thin almost to the point of gauntness; her face, high-cheekboned and once beautiful, now looked haggard. Her large and lovely gray eyes had the lost, slightly glazed expression of the habitual drunk. She was wearing a stunning black evening dress and a mink cape.

She entered the elevator and stabbed jerkily at the fifth-floor button. The car ascended. On the fifth floor, she weaved along the thickly carpeted corridor to her apartment. She reached out toward the bell, then remembered that her maid was on a few days' vacation. She swore under her breath and began to grope in her purse for the front-door key. She found it at last, aimed it at the lock, and lunged. She missed the opening by about half an inch, and tried again.

It was the sound of Alison's key tapping against the lock and sliding back and forth across its brass surface that alerted the man who was at that moment in the act of rifling the antique walnut bureau in Alison's living room.

The intruder gave a muffled gasp and for a second froze. Then he quickly extinguished the flashlight in his hand. The only illumination in the room was now the dim glow of the city from the windows, over which the drapes had not yet been drawn. This gave the man just enough light to snatch up a bulging canvas bag and flit silently to a tall closet in the corner. He slipped inside, drew the door almost shut after him and stood—motionless and silent as a statue, only the wild beating of his heart seeming, to him, likely to give away his presence.

Alison eventually got her front door open and, muttering crossly to herself, she entered the apartment. She flapped vainly at a wall switch, letting her cape fall from her shoulders to the floor as she did so. Then she lost interest and, leaving the living room unlit, made her way, as purposefully as her condition and the darkness allowed, in the direction of the kitchen. She went in, and this time was successful in switching on the light. She crossed to the refrigerator, opened it and took out a half-filled pitcher of martinis. She reached into a cupboard above the refrigerator, picked up a glass and poured a stiff drink. She downed it in one go, and as she lowered the glass her eye fell on a snapshot that was tacked onto a cork bulletin board next to the wall phone. It was a picture of her, smiling at a dark, slim, good-looking young man of about twenty-five.

Alison's expression changed, became harder. She slammed down her glass, stomped across to the phone, picked up the receiver and, after several fluffed attempts, eventually managed to dial a number. She stood with the receiver to her ear, listening to the ringing tone.

"Come on, come on, you creep," she muttered. "I want an explanation from you."

But the ringing remained unanswered, and after a minute, Alison angrily replaced the receiver. She turned to face the living room, and stopped dead. The kitchen light behind her showed, on the floor by her desk, an upturned drawer, with its contents spilled out over the carpet.

Alison's heart missed a beat. Then she stepped into the living room and switched on the light. She stood, staring, her still befuddled brain trying to take in what her eyes were seeing.

The room was in a shambles. Every drawer had been pulled out and turned upside down on the floor; the papers in her bureau had been scattered everywhere. Objects had been swept from tables and shelves. And—

Alison swung toward the wall on her right. In the center of it, the door of the safe hung wide open. Even from here she could see that her jewel box was missing.

Sheer anger overwhelmed Alison. She stamped her foot in almost childish temper.

"Damn you!" she said out loud. "Damn you, damn you!"

She then stood quite still for a few seconds, letting the scene of desolation sweep over her and into her.

Then she turned again and marched determinedly back to the kitchen. The shock had done something to sober her up—enough to know what she had to do. Again she lifted the receiver and dialed.

After a moment she said, "Police—I want to report a break-in."

Hardly were these words out of her mouth when she heard a strange rushing sound behind her. She swung around to see a slim figure in black sweater and pants and wearing a ski mask dashing across the room toward the front door. The intruder was carrying a canvas bag.

Alison gave a gasp of pure fury. If the figure had come toward her, she would probably have screamed, but the sight of the burglar trying to get away seemed to increase her anger. She dropped the receiver and started in pursuit.

If she hadn't been so imbued with Dutch courage, she'd never have tried it. But, although partly sobered up by the shock, her system was still full of alcohol—impaired in mind and body.

She caught up with the man just inside the door and flung herself on him—clawing, beating with her fists and kicking. The intruder managed momentarily to throw her off and tried to open the door. But again Alison came back, this time not striking at him, but clinging tight, attempting by sheer brute force to stop him.

It was a crazy ploy, and if she had been sober, Alison would have realized this. However, for a few moments it worked. Although thin, she was wiry, and tall for a woman; the burglar was slim and of no more than average height. They remained locked together, swaying from side to side, as the intruder attempted desperately to dislodge her. At first he did nothing but try to pry her loose and push her off, but as the seconds passed and still Alison clung to him, he clearly began to panic.

His breath started to come even faster, and he began to make little noises—half grunts, half whimpers—in his throat. Alison felt a surge of triumph. She was winning! If he'd just let go the bag, she'd release him—give him a chance to get away. She managed to gasp, "Drop it!" But he continued to cling to it like a limpet.

The end came suddenly. They barged into a small table just inside the door, on which stood a heavy bronze statuette. The man's eyes fell on it, and almost instinctively, he snatched it up with his free hand, raised it and crashed it down with all his force on Alison's head.

Like a puppet when the strings are released, she crumpled instantly to the floor. She lay quite still, not breathing.

For a moment the man was as motionless as his victim. Then he let the statuette fall from his gloved hand, carefully stepped over Alison's body and again approached the door. He bent, picked up her cape from the floor and stuffed it into his bag.

Next, he went right up to the door and put his ear against it. All was silent outside. He switched off the light, opened the door a crack and peered out. The corridor was deserted. He thanked his lucky stars that these swank places were solidly built and almost soundproof. Also that the rich kept to themselves.

He took a deep breath, slipped into the corridor and closed the door silently.

Around the ugly wound in Alison Brevard's temple the blood was already congealing. In the kitchen the telephone receiver swung slowly at the end of its cord and the martinis grew tepid in the pitcher.

Chapter Two

DR. Edmund Gerard was a soft-spoken, introspective man of about fifty-five. But he looked older than that, thought Jessica: he'd aged a good deal since she'd last seen him—before his wife's death. His hair was now gray. But it quite suited him; he looked much more like a distinguished academic than most of the other academics of her acquaintance, who often could be taken for farmers, prizefighters or gangsters.

He'd met Jessica at the Seattle-Tacoma airport in his own car and insisted on driving her to her hotel. He was apologetic about the hotel.

"I'm sorry I can't put you up at home, Jessica," he said as he eased his dark blue sedan out of the airport parking lot. "But the fact is, most of the house is shut up. I have no live-in staff—just a cleaning lady who comes in a few mornings a week—and I hardly ever eat at home. So it wouldn't be very pleasant for you. Still, I think you'll be quite comfortable at this hotel—and it *is* close to the campus."

"Frankly, Edmund, I'll be happier at a hotel. If I stayed with you, we'd spend far too many hours rehashing the old days."

"Probably true, but why shouldn't we?"

"Because, unfortunately, I have to work while I'm here."

"Work? You mean writing?"

"I'm afraid so. I have just about a week to finish my book."

She explained about her deadline. "I'm afraid there's not going to be much time for sightseeing," she ended.

"Oh, Jess, I'm sorry to drag you away at an awkward time. You should have explained it wasn't convenient to come right now."

"I very nearly did. But my vanity got the better of me. I couldn't throw away the chance of lecturing at a major university. But, of course, composing my lectures has put me even further behind with the book."

"I hate to think of your spending all your time here slaving away alone in a hotel room."

"Well, not all the time, and probably not alone. I think that for the first time in my life, I need a secretary. If I can get a girl to do the typing for me, three hours a day should enable me to meet the deadline. Do you think the hotel will have a secretarial service?"

"Probably, but I imagine it'll be quite expensive."

"Can't be helped, I'm afraid."

"Suppose we have a word with my secretary, Amelia Browne? I doubt she could spare the time personally, but she may be able to find someone for you. She's incredibly efficient herself, so I'm sure she wouldn't recommend a dud."

Jessica nodded. "Very well. Thank you."

"We can stop by the university and see her now if you like—before going to the hotel."

"Suits me," she said.

They found Amelia Browne in the anteroom to Edmund's office, seated at her desk, surrounded by dozens of bills, statements, credit card receipts and the like—all stacked into tidy piles. She was soberly dressed, her hair drawn into a neat bun. Her features were rather plain, but she had a pleasant, kindly expression.

Edmund introduced Jessica and explained her requirements.

Amelia nodded comprehendingly. "I'm sure we can help you, Mrs. Fletcher."

"I'd be very grateful. But I don't want to put you to any trouble. You seem to have your hands rather full." She indicated the paper-covered desk.

Edmund smiled. "Amelia handles all my accounts—for which I am eternally grateful. It's not part of her official duties, of course."

"It's my pleasure," Amelia said. She picked up a credit card receipt and held it up for Edmund to see. "By the way, Dr. Gerard, did you really order an inflatable raft from the White Saddle Sporting Goods Company?"

Edmund looked a shade embarrassed. "Just an impulse buy, I'm afraid. I had thoughts of taking a camping trip later in the year."

Amelia shook her head in mock despair. "It's a wonder he keeps any of his money," she said to Jessica.

Edmund chuckled. "You see, Jess, there she goes, acting like a wife again."

Jessica was looking at the secretary as Edmund said this, and she didn't miss the faintest flicker of distress which appeared for a moment in the woman's eyes. Then it was gone and Amelia was saying briskly: "I'll put the word out about the secretarial job. Some grad student will jump at it, believe me."

As they were walking through the campus on their way back to Edmund's car, Jessica asked, "Has Amelia been your secretary long?"

"Ten years, nearly eleven."

"You must find her invaluable."

"I don't know how I'd manage without her."

"You *do* realize she's in love with you?"

He stopped short. "*What* did you say?"

"Amelia's in love with you."

"Oh, don't be silly, Jess."

"There is none so blind as he who won't see."

"Stop quoting Jonathan Swift at me. No, Jess, you've got it wrong. She's fond of me, I think, and looks indul-

16

gently on my inefficiencies. But she tends to mother me, more than being in love with me—even though I must be ten years her senior.''

"No doubt you know best, Edmund," Jessica said quietly, in her most convincing meek-little-woman manner.

He eyed her suspiciously for a moment, but her expression was quite innocent.

Jessica found she had been allotted a very pleasant, spacious room, with a private bathroom and a patio that gave an excellent view of the city.

Edmund, who went up with her to inspect the accommodation, was quite anxious she should feel happy with it.

"Now, are you sure this is a room you can work in, Jess?" he asked. "If not, I can have you moved into a suite.''

"This'll be fine, Edmund. Honestly.'' She turned to the bellhop. "I'd like a typewriter, if that can be arranged.''

"Sure thing, ma'am. I'll see to it right away.'' He left the room.

"I'll leave you to get settled in now, Jess," said Edmund. "I hope you'll have dinner with me tonight.''

She shook her head regretfully. "Not tonight, Edmund, thank you. Tonight I'm going to bed early. I'm still on East Coast time, remember.''

"Of course. Tomorrow, then?''

"I'll look forward to it. I shall enjoy it more, too, having got my first lecture out of the way.''

He eyed her keenly. "You're not really nervous, are you?''

"Petrified.''

"There's no need, I promise you. We're always very nice to visiting lecturers at Sequoia.''

"I'm sure you are. That almost makes it worse. I can imagine everyone politely clapping afterward and whispering to each other, 'What on earth possessed Dean Gerard to invite this old fool?' ''

Edmund chuckled. "You'll be fine, Jess. Now, as you

know, it's scheduled for five tomorrow afternoon. Shall I pick you up here?"

"No need. I'll make my own way there. A good, bracing ten-minute walk before the lecture may be just what I need."

"As you like. Come straight to my office and I'll take you to the lecture room."

"If I don't chicken out on the way."

"You won't." He went to the door. "Good night, Jess."

"Good night, Edmund. And thanks for inviting me. I do appreciate it—whatever I may have said."

After he'd gone, Jessica unpacked her things, including her manuscript and notebooks, together with some typing paper (she always had the irrational feeling, whenever she traveled away from home, that she would be unable to buy things like this anywhere else). By the time she'd completed her unpacking, the bellhop had returned with a typewriter.

When he'd departed, well-tipped, Jessica phoned Room Service for some coffee and sandwiches, then took a shower. She'd finished by the time the waiter had arrived, and she watched TV while having her supper. Then, she decided, it was time for bed. She went to the bathroom, cleaned her teeth, came back—and suddenly realized that she felt completely alert and wide-awake. Really, how irritating! What should she do? Switch the TV on again, locate the most boring program she could find and rely on its soporific effect to send her to sleep? Or work? She didn't really enjoy working late at night (and on her personal time-clock, it was late). On the other hand, the more she could get ahead of her deadline, the better; and five hundred words down on paper tonight would mean she could take it a bit easier tomorrow.

She went to the table where she'd laid out her work things, sat down and picked up her pen.

It was half an hour later, and she was making slow but fairly satisfactory progress toward the Inspector's *dénouement*, when there came a loud knock on the door. Jessica looked up in surprise. She stood up, went to the door and called out: "Yes?"

A man's voice answered. "Mrs. Fletcher?"

"That's right."

"I'm here from the university."

Of course! They'd canceled her lecture. She'd expected something like this all along. With an emotion halfway between letdown and relief, and keeping the chain-lock in place, Jessica opened the door and peered out.

Standing in the corridor was one of the most handsome young men she had ever seen. He was about twenty-five, with black wavy hair and blue eyes. He smiled engagingly at her, showing two rows of pearly white teeth. While not especially tall, he was slim and lithe-looking.

Jessica was wondering if this was somebody kept on staff especially for the purpose of breaking bad news to visiting lady lecturers, when he said: "I've come about the job."

"I beg your pardon?"

"The secretarial job."

Jessica stared. "Oh . . ."

"My name's David Tolliver. I've brought a note from Miss Browne."

He handed her an envelope. Jessica took it, tore it open and read: *The bearer may not be exactly what you had in mind, but I'm sure you won't find anyone better in the whole of Seattle. However, if you're not satisfied, I'm certain there'll be plenty of other applicants. A.B.*

Jessica looked up from the note and studied the young man for a few seconds. Then she said, "You'd better come in."

She closed the door, unhooked the chain and opened the door again. David Tolliver strolled easily into the room. "Thank you." He glanced around appreciatively. "Nice room."

Jessica said: "Mr . . . er—"

"Tolliver."

"Mr. Tolliver, I was expecting . . ."

He smiled. "Someone in a skirt? Surely, Mrs. Fletcher, you're not going to hold my gender against me?"

"It's not that. I'd need to think about it. Actually, I wasn't expecting anybody so soon."

"Yes, I'm sorry about the hour. But I wanted to beat the crowd; and believe me, Mrs. Fletcher, they'll be lining up to work for you."

"Then in fairness I oughtn't to take on the first person who applies. I should give the others a chance . . ."

She trailed off as he walked casually across to her worktable and looked down at the papers strewn on it.

"That sounds fine," he said, "except it looks like you could use a typist right now."

"You mean you want to start tonight?"

"Why not? Look, let me give you an example of my skills." He picked up a page of her manuscript and handed it to her. "Have you finished polishing this?"

"Yes, I think so," Jessica said a little weakly.

"Good."

He sat down at the table, deftly inserted a sheet of paper into the typewriter, glanced at the page of writing and commenced typing with what seemed to her incredible rapidity. Then, without a pause in his typing, he said, "I don't mind competing as long as I'm given an equal footing. You'd be surprised how prejudiced some people can be—although it's more noticeable among male employers. Not that I've worked for that many men. I don't usually get the chance. Most of the time I end up working for women."

"I wonder why," Jessica said dryly.

He ignored this. "The question I'm most often asked is where I went to secretarial school, and of course, I didn't. I'm self-taught, but I promise you, Mrs. Fletcher, I'm fast and accurate. As a matter of fact, as you can see, I can even talk and type at the same time."

"Remarkable."

"I don't have to, of course. I *can* type in silence."

He continued to do so for another minute, then stopped,

tugged the paper from the machine and handed it to her with a flourish.

Jessica read it through and gave a nod. "Excellent. I congratulate you."

"I do one hundred and fifty words a minute shorthand, too."

"I wouldn't need that. Tell me, do you intend to make your living as a stenographer?"

He laughed. "Lord, no. I'm studying to be a journalist. But typing is sure a better way to raise tuition fees than slinging hash."

Jessica eyed him for a second or two.

"I only charge five dollars sixty an hour," he said hopefully.

Jessica smiled. "Believe it or not, that wasn't what I was thinking about. It's simply that I've never worked with a secretary of either sex yet, and I just feel I'd be more comfortable with a woman. . . . Of course, we won't be working together, as such. The typist will be working on stuff I've completed—and a lot of the time I won't be here . . ."

She suddenly came to a decision. "All right, Mr. Tolliver, you've got the job."

He looked pleased, but by no means surprised. She then realized that he'd never been in any real doubt that she would hire him.

"Great," he said. "Shall I start now?"

"No. Tomorrow morning."

"Not tonight? I can put in a couple of hours—"

"No, thank you," she said firmly. "Ten A.M. tomorrow will be fine . . . that is, if you don't have classes or anything."

He stood up. "Not tomorrow. I'll be yours to command."

"Very well. Ten o'clock it is."

She led him to the door and opened it. "Good night."

"Good night, Mrs. Fletcher. You've made a wise choice."

"I sincerely hope so," she said.

He strolled out, and she heard him go down the corridor, whistling softly to himself. She closed and bolted the door. A most self-confident young man. Overconfident, perhaps? But masses of charm. And certainly a first-rate typist—as Amelia had said. She only hoped he was reliable. And punctual.

Jessica went back to the table and sat down. But she suddenly found that she couldn't pen another word that night. What she had just written, plus what she'd done on the plane, made up a pretty good day's work, under the circumstances. And she was now sleepy.

She quickly tidied the papers on the table, and ten minutes later was in bed and asleep.

Chapter Three

JESSICA was up the next morning at six-thirty, and working on her book by seven. By ten o'clock she'd done another thousand words—a thousand good words, she thought.

David Tolliver was late. But only by two minutes, which didn't really count. He seemed eager to chat, but she put him immediately to work on typing what she'd written the previous day and this morning. The weather was fine and mild, and in order to get away from the clatter of the typewriter, she retired to a wicker chair on the patio to continue with the book.

He came out twice in the next two hours, to check on points of typography and punctuation; but by one o'clock she had, to her great satisfaction, completed her schedule for the day. She could knock off work now with a clean conscience.

David completed his typing at about the same time, and presented it to her with modest pride. She glanced through it quickly. "Oh, that seems excellent, David. Thank you. I'll proofread it later."

"There's no need," he said airily. "That can go straight to your publisher as it is."

"No doubt you're right, but I shall proofread it nonetheless. Now, about this"—she indicated the work she'd done in the last three hours—"can you come and do it this afternoon?"

" 'Fraid not. I have to study. But I could come in at

about five-thirty and do it. It shouldn't take me very long. Will that be all right?''

"That'll be fine. I won't be here myself, of course, but I'll tell them at the desk to let you have the key."

"Oh yes, your lecture. What time will you be back?"

"Not till fairly late. I'm going out to dinner afterward. Which means I won't see you again today; so I'd better pay you now." She started for her purse.

"No, please. I don't want any money until the job's done."

"Are you sure? It'd be no trouble—"

"I prefer it that way."

"As you wish. I'll see you tomorrow, then."

"Sure. Well, best of luck with your lecture." He made for the door.

"David?"

He turned. "Yes?"

"You hadn't been thinking of coming to the lecture, had you? I wouldn't want to stop you."

"Actually, no. I'm not really into mystery stories. My taste in literature runs more to Vonnegut and Hesse."

Jessica raised her eyebrows. "Detective stories and serious literature aren't mutually exclusive interests, you know. In fact, the genres often overlap."

"I realize that. But crime fiction just doesn't grab me. I've seen a little of the real thing, you see."

"I'm not without experience of it myself," Jessica said dryly.

"Yes, I know. Sorry. Didn't mean to be rude. But I believe in the complete truth always. Do forgive me."

"I should think you're incapable of being rude, David."

His face broke into a smile of devastating charm. "Thanks. You'll find all that stuff done when you come in tonight. And I'll see you tomorrow. 'Bye." He went out.

Jessica spent the early part of the afternoon going over her lecture notes—cutting, adding, amending and polishing. She had decided not to follow precisely Edmund's suggested program. He was quite happy about this.

At four-thirty she had a cup of tea in her room, changed, did her face and hair, and set off on the short walk to the campus. She felt just as she had at fourteen, going to school on the day of an important exam.

Jessica sat on a hard upright chair and fought the impulse to count the number of people in the room. Nearly a hundred, she guessed—more than she'd expected—and including at least half a dozen faculty members in the front row. Oh dear!

Edmund, at the rostrum, was introducing her. As far as she could tell, it was a very nice introduction—complimentary without being too flowery—but she was finding it hard to concentrate on his words.

At last, far too soon, she heard Edmund saying: "And so I'll take up no more time, but simply say, ladies and gentlemen—Jessica Fletcher."

He stepped back from the rostrum, smiled at Jessica and sat down. She stood and moved forward. There was a polite ripple of applause. She placed her notes on the rostrum, cast a brief glance down, took a deep breath and began.

"I was talking earlier to a young man who told me that crime fiction just didn't grab him. And I thought, if that is true, what a lot of great literature he's cut off from. For crime—and especially murder—has been a dominant element in world literature from time immemorial. It seems to be, along with sex and money, a subject of never-ceasing fascination. In fact, the three subjects are inextricably linked in fiction as in real life.

"The oldest murder story of all appeared in the fourth chapter of Genesis, where is recounted the murder of Abel by Cain. It's a short story, but one that contains all the vital elements: motive, crime, discovery and retribution. Certainly it lacks some of the later subtleties of the genre: the murderer makes no attempt to cover his tracks, sets no false alibi, doesn't try to throw the blame on anyone else or make a desperate last-minute attempt at escape. Although his only words of exculpation have passed into the language as a proverb, one feels that he never really expected to get away with it—perhaps because the investigator in the case was a more formidable opponent than Hercule Poirot, Philip Marlowe, or even Sherlock Holmes.''

A faint but decidedly warm chuckle eddied around the lecture room, and Jessica began to feel a little more confident. She continued.

''Maybe the Cain and Abel story lacks dramatic tension because it's true. Many people would deny this, but I feel that a story so brief, so bald, cannot be anything but true: no fiction writer could hope to get away with a tale so completely devoid of twists. Perhaps, therefore, *The Abel Murder Case* has no place in our lecture today and we should move on to what is undeniably fiction. I shall, in fact, jump centuries of ancient literature—a discussion of murder in classical Greek literature alone would require a whole series of lectures—and come to more modern times. I am tempted, I must admit, to begin my discussion of mystery fiction proper with the man who is probably the greatest crime writer of all time, William Shakespeare. I have never tallied the number of murders in Shakespeare. No doubt some savant has, and has published his findings, together with a full list of weapons used, types of poison employed, and a breakdown—in tabular form—of the various motives involved. If so, I haven't read it and I don't intend to. However, if anybody present does know the exact Shakespearean body count and would care to supply it, I'd be pleased if he'd do so now.''

Jessica paused and glanced with raised eyebrows along the row of academics in the front. There was an amused shaking of heads, which was followed by a guffaw from the student body. The laughter was entered into by at least one of the faculty members. This was a big, blond, ungainly-looking young man in his mid to late thirties, wearing a sports jacket and old jeans; although he sat with the staff, he looked more like an elderly student. He was already giving the strong impression of immensely enjoying the occasion. Jessica warmed to him.

To her great surprise, she was even beginning to enjoy herself. She took a sip of water and went on.

"I will, though, resist the temptation to discuss Shakespeare at length, merely digressing long enough to point out that a murder is the key event in many of the tragedies: the murder of Desdemona by Othello, and of Duncan by Macbeth, for instance. *Hamlet* has good claim to be regarded as one of the . . . well, I was going to say one of the first whodunits. That isn't quite correct—although in the early part of the play we don't *know* that Claudius murdered Hamlet's father, or, if so, whether Gertrude was an accomplice. It would be truer to call it one of the first of the how-will-he-be-exposed sub-genre of crime stories. In setting out to bring the truth to light, Hamlet himself becomes one of the first amateur detectives—and in being both of noble birth, and a scholar, may be regarded as the direct literary ancestor of Lord Peter Wimsey."

Jessica broke off and again glanced at the faculty members. "Now, there's a brand-new examination question, or essay subject, which I offer free of charge: 'Discuss the influence of *Hamlet* on the detective fiction of Dorothy L. Sayers.' "

She again waited for the laughter to die down before resuming.

"However, you are not here today to learn about a writer who no doubt has been discussed in this very room a great many times by people far better qualified than I. Before I leave the subject of Shakespeare, though, let me add that I am not, naturally, claiming that *Hamlet* and the other great tragedies are *merely* crime fiction. But then, *no* good crime fiction is *merely* crime fiction.

"Ellery Queen, of course, was well aware of this fact, when over thirty years ago he published his anthology *The Literature of Crime*—a book which elevated the prestige of the genre, containing as it did crime and mystery stories by, among others, authors as diverse as Sinclair Lewis, Galsworthy, Steinbeck, Faulkner, Hemingway, Twain, Huxley, Stevenson, Wells, Kipling and Charles Dickens."

She had read this list from her notes and now looked back at her audience.

"Yes, it makes you sit up, doesn't it? It did me when I first came across it. And perhaps you now understand more fully what I meant when I said that in taking no interest in crime stories, my young friend was cutting himself off from a considerable amount of great literature. Now, let us look at some of that literature more closely. . . ."

Three-quarters of an hour later Jessica arrived at her closing remarks. "Well, I hope I have demonstrated that the crime story occupies an honorable and important place in literature and that those who sneer at it only succeed in exposing themselves as possessed of an extremely provincial outlook. We have looked today at crime fiction of every kind. In many of these stories the identity of the criminal was known from the start; some of them in fact have been written from the criminal's viewpoint. Novels such as *A Gun for Sale* and *A Kiss Before Dying* contain little actual mystery element. Next time I plan to examine the development over the last century of the pure puzzle story—the whodunit—and I hope to prove that in the hands of a master this branch of fiction can provide a greater degree of intellectual stimulation in a single volume that a whole library of experimental or *avant-garde* novels. Thank you."

She stepped back and sat down. The applause broke out. Several students whistled their approval, while the faculty members clapped particularly warmly. Jessica got to her feet and gave a little bow. Then she sat down again.

Sitting beside her, Edmund was looking pleased as punch. As the applause finally died down, he turned to her with a grin.

"There you are, Jess. I knew you could do it."

At that moment the young lecturer from the front row came bustling up. "Mrs. Fletcher, my congratulations. That was fascinating."

"Why, thank you, er—"

Edmund said: "This is Professor Todd Lowery, Jess."

Lowery held out a big hand, which practically enveloped Jessica's. "I'm with the English department, Mrs. Fletcher," he said. "You've given me a fresh insight into crime fiction. I really think we ought to introduce a study of it into our curriculum."

"That would be very exciting."

"These things take a long time, of course, but I shall certainly push for it. Anyway, I look forward to the next lecture."

"Well, that will be more specialist and rather less literary."

"Then my wife will probably enjoy it even more. She's a great fan of the pure puzzle story. She wanted me to tell you how much she's enjoyed your first three books."

"Thank you. Is she here?"

"Emily? She was." Lowery glanced toward the door, where the crowds were milling out. "I don't see her right now. She's probably left."

"I'd like to meet her. No author can hear the words, 'I enjoy your books,' too often."

He smiled. "I'll tell her. I'm sure she'd love to speak with you next time. She's not one to push herself forward. I, of course—"

Various knots of people were still standing about the lecture room chatting; and, while speaking, Lowery had been glancing around, apparently still searching for a glimpse of his wife. Now he suddenly broke off. Jessica followed his gaze. Standing near one of the exits, and staring coolly and frankly at him, was a girl. She was an extremely attractive blue-eyed blonde of about thirty, with a quite stunning figure.

Lowery turned back to Jessica and got his train of thought under control with what was plainly something of an effort.

"I, of course, never have any inhibitions." He glanced at his watch. "Well, if you'll excuse me. . . . Can't wait for the next lecture. Goodbye."

He moved off toward the door by which the girl was standing.

At the same moment Edmund, who for the last minute had been engaged in urgent conversation with another faculty member, turned back to Jessica. They spoke together.

Edmund began: "Jessica, I'm afraid—"

Jessica said, "Edmund, that wouldn't be—"

They both stopped. "After you," said Edmund.

"That wouldn't be Emily Lowery, I suppose?"

For a second he looked blank. "Who? Where?"

"The playmate of the month—standing by the door."

He stared in the girl's direction. "Good Lord, no. That's Jack Schroeder's wife. Lila, I think her name is. Emily's rather a demure little creature."

At that moment Lowery reached the door and walked straight out into the corridor without glancing sideways at the girl. She, on the other hand, kept her eyes fixedly upon him; and as soon as he was through the door she turned and followed him out.

"Who's Jack Schroeder?" Jessica inquired.

"The swimming coach. I believe they're living apart now."

"She's not studying English, I suppose?"

"Oh no. Hardly the type, I'd imagine. I'm surprised to see her here, actually. What is this, Jess?"

"Oh, nothing, Edmund. What were you going to say?"

He looked a little awkward. "I'm terribly sorry, but I'm afraid I've got to let you down."

"How do you mean?"

"I've just been told we have a crisis. Nothing that need concern you. But we have to hold an emergency faculty meeting. I'm afraid I can't take you to dinner after all."

"Please, Edmund, no apologies necessary."

"But what will you do? I'm sure I could find someone who'd be delighted to escort you—"

"No, please don't think of it. I'll be delighted to have a quiet meal in my hotel room, watch TV for an hour or two, and turn in early. I've had a long day."

"Well, if you're sure. Can I get you a taxi?"

"Don't go to the bother. I'll be glad to walk."

"Okay. I'll be able to make it tomorrow for sure."

"I'll hold you to it."

"Thanks for your understanding, Jess. I'll call you."

He hurried from the room. Jessica noticed for the first time that a number of students were hanging around a few yards away, eyeing her diffidently. She smiled at them, and they came near her. A few were holding copies of her books, which they wanted autographed. She remained with them for about a quarter of an hour, discussing mystery novels and answering their questions. (Though she was, as always, unable to answer the most persistently repeated inquiry: how she thought up her plots. A weak and rather apologetic "they just come" was about the best she could do.)

When the students dispersed—all promising to attend the next lecture—Jessica made her way back to her hotel. She felt physically drained and was rather relieved not to be going out with Edmund. Though she did feel quite elated about the lecture. It had gone much better than she'd anticipated, and she was far happier now about the other lectures. If this one had been a flop, it would have been awful having the prospect of two more hanging over her.

She reached her hotel and asked at the desk for her key. To her surprise she was informed that Mr. Tolliver had not yet returned it. The work must have taken him longer than he'd anticipated, she thought as she went up in the elevator.

However, when she entered the room, the typewriter was covered and beside it lay a neat little pile of typescript. She went over and glanced at it. Yes, it was this morning's work. But there was no sign of David.

Then she noticed that the patio lights were on. She went out.

David looked up at her with a slow, lazy smile and got to his feet. In his hands was a copy of *The Corpse Danced at Midnight*.

"Hi," he said.

"Hello, David. I didn't expect to find you still here."

"Well, don't worry. I'm not charging for my time now. I had to hang on and find out how the lecture went."

"Quite well, I think—thanks partly to you."

"Me?"

"Your remarks about crime fiction gave me an idea for a new opening. Then I was able to spend a good part of the hour shooting you down in flames. There was quite a big audience and they seemed to enjoy it."

He looked hurt. "That was a bit severe, wasn't it? I'll be the laughingstock of the campus tomorrow."

"Don't worry. I didn't mention your name."

"Well, that's a relief. Guess I'd better come to the next lecture."

"I thought you weren't into crime fiction."

"I am now."

"Since when?"

"Since I started this." He held up the book. "It's really good."

"Thank you." Her voice was a little cool.

"No, I mean it: these characters are real. They're alive."

"So a few people have said—including one or two eminent critics."

"Oh, I never read book reviews. I prefer to make up my own mind. And about this book I have. I want to apologize for what I said earlier. It must have sounded pretty pompous."

Jessica smiled. "Just a little."

"The work's all done," he said.

"So I noticed. Very nice."

"I didn't expect you back yet. I thought you were going out to dinner."

"I was stood up."

"Shame!"

"No, not really. Dr. Gerard had an emergency meeting. He offered to find a substitute."

"But no one measured up to your standards. Would I?"

She blinked. "I'm sorry, I—"

"Would I measure up? Would you have dinner with me?"

"Oh, David, that's very sweet of you; but really, there's

no need for you to be kind to a middle-aged woman. I'm sure you have a nice girl waiting somewhere.''

"No, honestly, I haven't. I'd like to take you to dinner. I'd like to talk. Truly.''

Jessica looked at him thoughtfully, then glanced at her watch. It was after seven, and she'd eaten nothing since a very light lunch at one.

"Well, actually I was going to have something sent up. And frankly, I don't think my digestive tract could handle pizza and beer—or whatever it is you young people eat nowadays.''

"*Those* young people eat pizza and beer. But I'd prefer a Châteaubriand anytime. How about it?''

Jessica's eyebrows went up. "David, are you sure you can afford that?''

"Quite sure I can't. But you can.''

She stared at him speechlessly for a moment. He grinned back. In manner, he reminded her very much of her nephew Grady, who could always twist her around his finger. She suddenly laughed.

"Go downstairs and wait for me in the bar. I have to change.''

"Great.'' He seemed genuinely delighted—though probably only at the prospect of getting a free meal. "I'll phone for a reservation somewhere. I think I know just the place.''

The *place* he knew, Jessica guessed, was probably the most expensive restaurant in Seattle. It had the lot: thick carpets; exquisite linen and silver; fine china; quiet, rapid and highly obsequious waiters. It also possessed a very romantic atmosphere, with candles and soft music. The rest of the clientele, in fact, seemed to consist almost exclusively of obviously rich young lovers.

Seated at a corner table with David, Jessica felt decidedly out of place. While they were sipping their aperitifs, she said as much. "I keep thinking everyone's staring at me.''

"Well, you're famous.''

"My face isn't. And I guarantee none of this crowd was at the lecture."

"I guess not. They're probably staring at *me*—with envy in their hearts."

"Oh, David, that's not just transparent; it's corny."

"Only the words, not the thought."

"Don't be silly."

"Okay." He put down his glass. "Let's say I *was* being silly. Those guys are not particularly envious of me—because, truth to tell, they probably haven't given us a thought. But they ought to be. Quite frankly, most of the girls in here are *stupid*. They can't talk. The truth is, I have a middle-aged psyche bottled up in this twenty-five-year-old body. I don't enjoy the company of my bubble-headed female contemporaries. I do enjoy yours. I can't remember when I've had such a good time."

"I'm sure that's not true."

"It is. Honestly." He raised his glass. "Jessica, thank you for coming. To you."

He drank. She said, a little awkwardly, "Thank you."

He lowered his glass. "Do you mind if I call you Jessica?"

"Not at all."

"I just can't think of you as 'Mrs. Fletcher.' I already feel so close to you—as though I've known you for years. And getting to know you has really meant a lot to me. I want you to believe that."

She took a deep breath. Something had to be said. "David, this is beginning to sound a bit silly. I'm old enough to be your—"

He put his hand on hers, effectively cutting her off. "To be my friend," he said softly. "Why don't we leave it at that?"

At that moment, rather to her relief, the waiter appeared with their food.

The meal, if not outstanding, was acceptable, though Jessica didn't enjoy it as much as she might have. She continued to feel uncomfortable and to imagine that eyes were on her. Seeming to sense this, David turned the conversation almost immediately to her books. On this topic he displayed a lively interest. His questions were intelligent; he never once asked her how she thought up her plots; and she gradually lost her self-consciousness and was eventually chatting fluently.

Too fluently, she suddenly realized when they were drinking their coffee. "Now, that's more than enough about me and my work," she said. "I know very little about you—apart from your plans to be a journalist. Tell me more about yourself."

He shrugged. "There's little to tell. It's all very dull, I'm afraid. For the last several years it's mostly been a question of long hours of hard work."

"Parents?"

"Both dead, for many years."

"I'm sorry. Girl friends?"

"I told you I don't often seek the company of young girls."

"Ah, but that can't always have been the case. You had to discover you didn't like their company, didn't you?"

"That's true. There have been girls, of course. But nobody I want to talk about, if you don't mind."

His voice had gone suddenly cold. Jessica suspected he was in the throes of getting over an unhappy romance, perhaps a broken engagement. Had a girl treated him badly? That would account for his contempt for what he'd called his female contemporaries. In which case it was no doubt a very temporary phenomenon.

She changed the subject. "One thing you said interested me."

He smiled. "Only one? Oh dear."

"One thing in particular. That you'd had a bit to do with real-life crime. What exactly did you mean?"

"Oh, that. Don't get me wrong. I didn't mean I've had much personal involvement. It's just that I spend quite a lot of time down at the courthouse. I listen to the cases, take a shorthand notebook and try to write an interesting report of the case. It was a special-studies project in the first place, but it seemed such good practice that I kept on with it. I even got permission to talk to some of the prisoners. I've written up some of my interviews with them and tried to sell them. Without luck so far."

Jessica nodded. "I see. Must have been interesting. I'm afraid I was imagining—"

"That I'd been involved in some horrible crime . . . suspect in a murder case, or something?"

"Something like that, yes."

"Nothing so dramatic. As I said, I've lived an extremely dull life. Until tonight, that is."

"David . . . !"

"Sorry—sorry. I was forgetting you don't like people to say nice things about you, however true they happen to be."

"I wouldn't go that far. What I don't like is flattery."

He looked hurt. "That wasn't flattery. This is quite a thrill for me. I'm enjoying myself enormously. Don't spoil it for me."

"I'm sorry. No doubt I'm oversensitive. Forgive me."

He smiled. "Nothing to forgive."

At that moment the waiter sidled up and discreetly laid their check on the table next to David. Jessica reached out for it. "I'll take that."

"No, you don't," said David, scooping up the check. "I was only joking. You didn't really think I'd let you pay, did you?"

"David, you must. I can afford it. You admitted you couldn't."

"I can't afford lots of things that I do all the time."

He took out his wallet and extracted a hundred-dollar bill. She couldn't help noticing that there were several others in the wallet. He handed the money, with the check, to the waiter, saying with a grin, "*Don't* keep the change."

"No, monsieur."

The waiter departed, and David looked back at Jessica, returning his wallet to his pocket as he did so. "I never claimed to be starving."

"No, I know."

"Fact is, I allow myself one meal in a good restaurant each semester. This has been the one for this semester."

"All the same, I'm not happy about it. I would never have come if I'd known you were going to pay for me."

"Well, of course, if you'd like to return the compliment later in the week, I'll be happy to let you pick up the tab."

"That won't help to restore your bank balance."

"No, but it'll do wonders for my digestion. And yours, if I may say so. I bet you live on snacks most of the time. It's not good for you."

"Now don't *you* start mothering *me*." She glanced at her watch. "If you don't mind, I think I'd like to go now. It's been a long day."

He looked disappointed. "Sure you wouldn't like to go somewhere? I know some good night spots. One where the local mobsters hang out. Might give you some material."

"Thank you, no. I don't write about mobsters, anyway. I write about nice, polite middle-class murderers."

A few minutes later, outside, David opened the passenger door of his car for Jessica to get in. It was a long, low red sports model. Jessica surveyed it. She was not greatly interested in automobiles; earlier in the evening the only thing that had struck her about it was how very difficult it was to get out of. Now she realized that it must be a pretty expensive model.

"This is a very nice car," she said.

"A reflection of the man."

He bowed and held the door wide for her. She was about to enter when a large black sedan came along the street and drew up within a couple of inches of David's front fender. He looked annoyed. "He might give me a bit of room to—"

He broke off as two men emerged from the sedan and approached them with a purposeful air. They were tall and burly, dressed in dark suits. The slightly older one was black, and it was he who spoke.

"David Tolliver?"

"Yes."

"I'm Lieutenant Andrews, Seattle P.D." He flashed

37

some identification. "Sir, would you mind accompanying us to headquarters? We have a few questions we'd like to ask you."

David was looking bewildered. "Yes, I would mind. Questions about what?"

Andrews shot a quick glance in Jessica's direction. "It won't take long, Mr. Tolliver."

"Look," David said, "if you've got something to ask, ask it, so I can get this lady back to her hotel. Tell me what this is about."

Andrews gave a slight shrug. "All right. It concerns the murder of Alison Brevard."

David drew his breath in sharply. "Why do you want to speak to me about that?"

"You were . . . er, acquainted with the lady."

"Yes—but so were dozens of other people."

"You had a date with her the night she was murdered."

"No." David gulped. "Well, yes . . . I mean, originally I did. But I wasn't able to keep it. I canceled."

"Did you, Mr. Tolliver?" Before David could answer, Andrews went on: "My information is that you knew the lady well. She had your picture in her apartment. Now, are you prepared to come with us, or do I have to put you under arrest?"

"Seems I have no choice," David said bitterly. "What about my car?"

"You can drive it to headquarters. The sergeant will ride with you."

"But I can't just leave this lady—"

"She can come if she wants to, or we can get her a cab now."

David turned helplessly to her. "Jessica . . ."

He suddenly seemed very young: helpless, forlorn and rather frightened. Jessica came to a rapid decision. "I'd like to come."

He looked grateful. "Are you sure? It won't be very pleasant. . . ."

"I've had some experience with police stations."

"Okay," Andrews said, "get in the car."

"Lieutenant, you may not have noticed that Mr. Tolliver's car is a two-seater," Jessica said. "If the sergeant is riding in it, there won't be room for me. I'm afraid I shall have to travel with you."

He hesitated, then gave a curt nod. "As you like. Let's go."

Chapter Four

FOR the first couple of minutes Jessica and Andrews traveled in silence. It was she who spoke first.

"My name is Fletcher—Jessica Fletcher."

"Pleased to meet you." Then the name seemed to strike a chord. He said, "The writer?"

"Yes."

He gave her a quick sideways look. "And amateur detective?"

"No," she said firmly.

"I thought . . . I mean, surely you've been—"

"Other people keep regarding me as an amateur detective. In fact, on three separate occasions—in New York, in Maine and in Los Angeles—I have been asked by police officers to help them. I didn't want to, but I really had no choice."

"Well, I'll tell you one thing, ma'am. You won't be asked to help in Seattle."

"Good. I wouldn't have time, anyway. I have to deliver two lectures at Sequoia University *and* finish a novel in less than a week."

"Fine. Then we understand each other." He paused; then: "How d'you think up your plots?" he asked.

Jessica sat on a bench in the waiting room at police headquarters for over an hour. People came and went around her. Nobody spoke much. Some faces were bewildered, others anxious, most merely blank. One old man slept solidly, snoring quietly now and again. At last for the twentieth time the door opened and Jessica, glancing wearily toward it, saw David standing there. He looked tired, but was smiling. She got to her feet and went to him.

"David, are you all right?"

"Fine—and free to go."

"Oh, good."

They went out. "Jessica," he said, "thanks for waiting. I'm terribly sorry to put you through this. Now let's get you home, pronto."

In the car he said, "It was just routine, really. They're talking to everyone who knew Alison. I think I was number forty-eight on a list of fifty."

"You knew her well?"

"Not really. I was just one of the dozens of men friends she had."

"But you had had a date with her the night she was killed."

"Well, we'd dine together once in a while. She liked to talk. That was all there was to it. This time I'd had to cancel—pressure of work."

"You *did* know she'd been murdered?"

"Only what I read in the papers. Seems she surprised some burglar in her apartment. Jewelry and a mink were stolen. She must have put up a struggle: the police found black wool threads under her nails—probably from his sweater."

"I see. How was she killed?"

"Hit over the head with some sort of statuette. Must have died almost instantly."

"It must have been a shock when you heard about it."

"Of course. But somehow . . . well, it wasn't all that much of a *surprise*, if you know what I mean. Alison was one of life's victims, I'm afraid. Anyway, I'm out of it now, thank God."

Jessica didn't speak. There were dozens of questions she wanted to ask, but she resisted firmly. It was really nothing to do with her. Nothing at all. . . .

Ten minutes later David dropped her outside her hotel.

She refused his offer to escort her to her room, and stood on the sidewalk watching his sports car as it roared away. As it did so, a black sedan—very similar to that driven by Andrews—which had pulled up fifty yards down the street as she alighted, started moving again and sped off in the same direction.

Jessica went indoors. She was almost certain the sedan had been behind them when they drove away from police headquarters. Somehow she doubted very much if David Tolliver was "out of it," after all.

The next day Jessica again started work on her book early and, with just a short break for lunch, kept hard at it all morning and afternoon. By six o'clock, to her intense satisfaction, she'd got well ahead of her schedule: the end of the book was now just a few days off, and she could afford to take it a bit easier, as a couple of hours' work a day should see her finished in time.

Edmund had phoned to confirm their dinner engagement, but she had no other appointments before then; and as David was not coming for another typing session until the next day (he was so fast he could easily catch up with her), she was rather surprised, while rereading her day's work, to hear a tap on the door. She went across and opened it, keeping the chain in place. Lieutenant Andrews was standing outside.

"Why, good evening, Lieutenant." She unhooked the bolt. "What can I do for you?"

"I'd like a word, ma'am, if it's not inconvenient."

"Come in."

She stepped back and he came into the room.

"What's this about?" she asked.

"David Tolliver."

"Don't say he's been arrested?"

"No . . . not yet."

"Not yet? Surely you don't really think he killed that woman?"

"I can't comment on that, Mrs. Fletcher."

"Why are you here, Mr. Andrews?"

He hesitated. "Frankly—to give you a bit of advice."

"Oh? And what's that?"

"Stay away from David Tolliver."

Jessica's eyebrows nearly disappeared into her hair. "Really—isn't that rather presumptuous?"

He shrugged. "Maybe. Sometimes it's our duty, though, just to give a friendly warning. Now, I know he's a good-looking, charming young guy; and I'm sure to a lady like you it's very flattering to have someone like that being attentive, paying compliments, making you feel—feel, er—"

"*Young*, Lieutenant? Is that the word you're groping for?"

"Let's say *younger*, ma'am."

Jessica took a deep breath. "Just what do you imagine is the relationship between David and me?"

"It's hardly for me to say."

"Well, I'll tell you. I arrived in this city two days ago. I hired him to type my manuscript—he's a marvelous typist. Yesterday evening Dean Gerard of Sequoia University had to beg off our dinner engagement. David offered to take his place. And that is the extent of our relationship."

"Naturally, I accept that, Mrs. Fletcher. But I assure you that's not all Tolliver has in mind. And he's bad news. I'm just warning you—for your own good."

"I think I'm old enough to look after myself, thank you."

"I hope so, ma'am."

"Lieutenant," Jessica said slowly, "I'm not a bad judge of people. David has his faults: rather too much self-confidence and a tendency to flattery. But I like him. Now, it's quite obvious you suspect him of murder—I saw the police car tailing us last night. But I am sure of one thing—that he is incapable of beaning somebody with a statuette. And I'll wager you ten dollars that he did not kill Alison Brevard."

Andrews gave a slow smile. "I might take you up on that, if I didn't figure it was kind of unethical: the thought of such riches might make me press too hard for a conviction."

43

She sighed in exasperation. "I cannot understand why you suspect him—as obviously you haven't any *firm* evidence, or you'd never have let him go. He didn't know the woman well. She was just a casual acquaintance."

Andrews uttered a snort of derision. "Casual acquaintance, my foot! Mrs. Fletcher, they were lovers. She was paying his tuition fees. She bought him that sports car he took you out in last night."

Jessica stared at him. "Are you sure?"

"Sure I'm sure."

She rallied. "In that case, why would he want to kill her?"

"Who knows? Maybe she wouldn't come across with enough dough and he decided to help himself to her jewels. Remember, he had made a date with her. That way he'd be sure of getting her out of the apartment. But he didn't turn up for the date. Where was he? He says studying in his room, but there's no confirmation of that."

"He canceled the date in advance."

"That's not our information. According to a bartender, and a cabbie who drove her home, she said she'd been stood up—her date hadn't shown. And at first she was hopping mad about it. Then she had a few drinks and became maudlin."

Jessica was thoughtful for a few moments. Then she said, "Well, Lieutenant, maybe I've been deceived by David. He has tremendous charm, and perhaps I let that fact blind me to all his faults. He *could* be a bit unscrupulous where money or women are concerned. He could be a fortune-hunter. But I'm still certain that he couldn't commit a violent murder."

"Even if she caught him robbing her apartment and was going to call the police? So he could see his whole future life being ruined?"

"I don't believe so, no. I think his reaction in that situation would be to run."

The lieutenant shrugged again. "Well, we'll see. Anyway, I've done what I felt I had to. You're a distinguished visitor to our city, Mrs. Fletcher. I wouldn't want any harm to come to you."

"I appreciate your concern, Lieutenant, and I assure you I shall take every precaution to avoid coming to harm."

"You do that, ma'am." He moved to the door. "I'll say good night."

"Good night, Mr. Andrews. And thank you. And by the way—"

"Yes?"

"You can still have that bet, if you want it."

Andrews gave a grin. "I'll pass this time, thanks."

He went out.

Jessica sat down slowly. Her mind was in a whirl.

"Edmund," Jessica said, "how well do you know David Tolliver?"

"Well, it's impossible to get to know many of my students as well as I'd like to. I suppose I must say *not very*."

They were just finishing dinner. The restaurant was by no means as posh as the one David had taken her to, but the food was considerably better and the atmosphere far more comfortable. They had been chatting as only very old friends could chat for an hour, but at last Jessica dredged up the subject which had been constantly at the back of her mind since Andrews' visit. Now she said: "Well, from what little you *do* know, what do you think of him?"

Edmund considered. "He's bright, intelligent; a good student, certainly—though I'm not sure he works quite as hard as he should."

"What about his character—I mean his moral character?"

"Well, he's never been caught cheating in exams. That's about all I can tell you. Why do you ask?"

"You know Amelia sent him along to do my typing?"

"Yes, she mentioned it. Isn't he satisfactory?"

"As a typist, very. I think I'd better tell you the whole thing."

She did so. Edmund listened closely. When she'd fin-

45

ished, he shook his head slowly. "David Tolliver a murderer? I can't believe it, Jess."

"Neither can I. But there are things that worry me."

"Such as?"

"That evening we were talking about crime. He'd mentioned earlier that he'd had a bit to do with it. I asked him what he meant, and he told me about his journalistic exercises—reporting court cases, interviewing prisoners. He more or less specifically stated he'd never been personally involved in a crime."

"Well, he hadn't then, had he? It was only after that the police took him in."

"But surely it would be natural, almost inevitable, when we were talking like that about crime, to mention that an acquaintance of his had just been murdered?"

Edmund looked pensive. "Not necessarily. I can think of two reasons why he might not."

"What are those?"

"Suppose he *had* stood the woman up that night, and that as a result she'd gone home alone much earlier than expected—and been murdered. Don't you think he might be feeling terribly guilty about it?"

Jessica nodded. "He certainly might. All I can say is that he didn't seem to feel the slightest guilt."

"He may be a very good actor."

"Oh, I'm sure he is. What's the other reason?"

"Embarrassment. If he was being more or less kept by an older woman, he might well have hoped to keep the fact quiet."

"But he'd realize that was impossible. The police always dig up things like that."

"I'm not suggesting he hoped to keep it from the *police*."

"Just from *me*?"

"Yes. It was very bad luck that they happened to pick him up for questioning when he was actually with you."

"Why?"

"Well, wouldn't it be likely to make you less inclined to, er . . ."

Jessica was never slow on the uptake. "You mean he's looking for another meal ticket?"

"In a sense, perhaps. And if you knew that the last meal ticket had been murdered in circumstances which might throw suspicion on David, you'd probably—or so he'd imagine—want to steer clear of him."

"But he couldn't possibly cast me in the role of meal ticket. I'm only in town for a week."

"I said meal ticket *in a sense*. David will be looking for a job soon. He might hope—if he made himself very useful to you while you were here, and was extremely charming and attentive—that you'd take him on as a full-time secretary."

"But he wants to be a journalist."

"Maybe he doesn't. Maybe he just wants to write. And being secretary to you, Jess, would be a lovely job for a would-be writer. You wouldn't be a hard taskmaster, you'd read his work, advise him, introduce him to your publishers. It would be a perfectly legitimate aspiration—but one which would make him very wary of mentioning any association with Alison Brevard and the circumstances of her death."

Jessica nodded thoughtfully. "Yes, Edmund, that all makes very good sense. It was a possibility that hadn't occurred to me."

"Does it make you feel a bit better about him?"

"Oh, yes. Though I still find the idea of his living on that woman highly distasteful."

"Well, it's purely his business, I suppose. Now . . . let's talk about something else."

"Like what?"

"Like you. And your books. You know, we've hardly mentioned them."

"It's been a nice change not to."

"Oh, then I won't press the topic. But just tell me one thing, will you?"

"What's that?"

"How on earth do you think up your plots?"

*   *   *

Jessica opened the door of her hotel room and stopped abruptly. The light was on inside. Surely, she hadn't left it on. The next second she heard the rattle of the typewriter. She went right in. Seated at the worktable, his hands racing over the keys, was David.

He looked up, stopped typing and gave a grin. "Hi."

"David, how did you get in here?"

"The maid let me in. She knew I was working for you."

"I thought you weren't coming today."

"I found I had an hour or two to spare. I figured I'd make a start."

"It's very late." She crossed to the table and glanced at the papers on it. Her eyebrows rose. "You don't seem to have done very much."

"No, unfortunately, the typewriter's been playing up. I've been fiddling with it for ages with my little pocket screwdriver." He produced this. "I think the machine's okay now."

"You shouldn't have bothered. I'm sure the hotel would provide a replacement."

"I didn't realize it would take so long. I suppose you don't want me to keep at it?"

"Hardly. I'm going to bed as soon as possible. So I think you'd better leave right away."

He frowned. "Jessica, you seem quite different tonight. Very cool. Why?"

"Well, for one thing I don't like people coming into my room uninvited."

"I'm sorry. It seemed like a good idea at the time."

"Very well. We won't say any more about it."

He stood up. "There's more to it than that, isn't there? Jessica, have the police been talking to you about me?"

"Why should you think that?"

"Something that lieutenant said. He more or less warned me to keep away from you. I made it obvious I wouldn't, and he talked about 'taking steps.' "

"As a matter of fact, he did come to see me."

"To warn you I was a danger to the entire female populace of Seattle?" He spoke bitterly.

"He didn't go quite as far as that."

"Jessica, I didn't kill Alison Brevard."

"I never thought you did. But you did lie to me about your involvement with her. For one thing, she bought you that car."

He gave a groan. "Is that what he told you?"

"Isn't it true?"

"Technically it's true. But it's thoroughly misleading to put it like that. What he didn't tell you is that Alison had wrecked my old car."

Jessica frowned. "She was driving it?"

"No, it was parked at the curb. She slammed into it head-on. It was a total write-off. That was the first time I met her."

"Was she hurt?"

"No, just badly shaken. And very drunk. She begged me not to notify the police or the insurance people, and swore she would replace my car. I found out later she had quite a record of accidents and couldn't afford another one. Eventually, I agreed. Her car wasn't too badly damaged, and she was in such a state I drove her home. The next day that sports car was delivered to me, fully paid for. I nearly fell over. Of course I went straight over to thank her. Our friendship started there."

"I see." Jessica nodded slowly. "Well, it certainly puts a new complexion on the story. But Mr. Andrews also says Alison was paying your tuition fees."

"No!" He was vehement. "She loaned me four hundred and fifty dollars. My final tuition payment was due and I was broke. I paid it back three weeks ago—out of money I earned typing other students' theses."

Jessica gazed at him. His face was flushed, and it was almost impossible not to believe him. She said, "If those are the facts, I was misled and I apologize. I take it your financial situation is now improved?"

He looked blank for a moment, then smiled. "Oh, you mean my loaded wallet the other night? Well, only very temporarily. Fact is, I had a hot tip on a horse. I scraped twenty-five bucks together, and my choice romped home at twenty-to-one. That's the only day for years I've had that much cash on me. Our dinner was a celebration. I just thought you wouldn't approve if you knew where the money came from.''

Jessica smiled too. ''I've put the odd dollar on a horse from time to time myself.'' Then she asked, ''Why do you think the police suspect you?''

He shrugged. ''Who knows? She had my picture in her apartment, but it was only a snapshot somebody took of us together; she pinned it up by the phone in her kitchen. I suppose people had seen us together, too. But there was nothing to it. We weren't in love. I liked her. She could be delightful company. When she was sober, that is. Which wasn't very often. We had dinner a few times; that was the extent of it. She'd had dozens of male friends. I'll admit I think she liked me. I grew fond of her. But I wouldn't have gone on seeing her if I hadn't been rather sorry for her—and, second, felt I owed her something in return for the car and the loan.''

''Did you stand her up the night she was killed?''

''No. I phoned the day before, telling her I had to work and couldn't make it.''

''Why do you think she *said* she'd been stood up?''

''Probably forgot I'd called. She was definitely tipsy at the time. I suppose I should have called again, to make sure the message had sunk in; but there'd have been no guarantee of catching her sober.'' He paused. ''You do believe me, don't you?''

''That you didn't kill her? Yes, I do. But I can see the police point of view. It's a shame you don't have an alibi for the time of the murder.''

''But not surprising. It's far from unusual to find a student studying alone in his room at night.''

''Well, David, I told the lieutenant you could never kill somebody in that way, and I stick to that. And I'm sure you have nothing to worry about. After all, if a person hasn't committed a crime, there's no way the police can prove he did."

"Maybe, but unless they find the real guy, there'll always be that suspicion hanging over me."

"I'm sure they'll find the murderer."

"I wish I was. Jessica, would you help? You've trapped a few killers already."

"Oh, David, what could I do? I was personally involved in those cases. I knew the victims. And I was asked to help by the police. Andrews has already made it quite clear I won't be asked to help here."

"Well, will you take an interest? Read about the case, talk about it, and *think* about it? You just might come up with an idea."

"Yes, David, I'll do that. I'll do anything I can to help clear you, though I'm sure it won't be much."

He gave her his devastating smile. "Thanks, Jessica, I do appreciate it." He looked at his watch. "Now, if you're sure you don't require my services, I'll be off."

"Quite sure, thanks."

"Tomorrow morning?"

"That'll be fine."

"Good night, then."

"Good night, David."

He left the room. Jessica went to the door and bolted it. Then she sat down on the bed and stared thoughtfully at the floor. She just didn't know what to make of the boy. She didn't believe he was a killer. But she still wasn't at all sure, in spite of his explanations, that Alison Brevard hadn't been keeping him. She thought he would be capable of exploiting a woman for his own ends.

Further, why had he been in her room tonight? Had he come to work, and was the story of the broken typewriter true? Or had that just been an excuse? What could he have wanted here? He knew she'd be out.

Jessica's eyes wandered around the room—and suddenly alighted on her attaché case. It was on the floor between the bed and the dressing table. And one of the catches was open. She was sure—*almost* sure—she hadn't left it like that. Had David been snooping? He wouldn't have found much of interest—mostly work notes, letters from her publisher; one from Edmund regarding this trip; another from Abby confirming her visit to Kentucky; a few other items. But had a search through her things been the sole purpose of his visit? If so, to what end? Was he simply one of the types who liked to store up information about people, just hoping it might come in useful? She could hardly believe it of David.

Perhaps she had left the catch improperly fastened. She didn't really think so, but she had to give David the benefit of the doubt.

Jessica sighed, put the whole thing out of her mind and went to bed.

Chapter Five

JESSICA'S second lecture was just as successful as the first. Word about her performance had got around, and the seats were packed. "We'll have to find a larger room for your third," Edmund murmured as he surveyed the audience. She got to her feet with more confidence this time, and at the end felt reasonably pleased. The applause certainly was highly enthusiastic.

Afterward there was a surprise. She discovered the faculty had prepared a reception for her. About thirty staff members were present, and she was amazed to find how much interest there was in the mystery genre, even from the science faculty. At the beginning Todd Lowery was present with his wife—a quiet, shy little woman—but they left together for home fairly early.

The reception was drawing to a close when someone tapped her on the shoulder and told her she was wanted on the telephone. She was taken out and led to a pay phone in the corridor.

She picked up the receiver. "Hello?"

A woman's voice said, "Mrs. Fletcher?"

"Yes."

"Look, you don't know me, but I'm a friend of David Tolliver, and I can prove he didn't kill that woman."

"Who are you?" Jessica asked sharply.

"My name's not important. Now just listen. We have to meet."

"You know where I'm staying?"

"No. We can't be seen together. Get this: there's an abandoned warehouse—Number 33—down by the Harbor Island docks. I'll meet you there at ten o'clock tonight."

"Whoever you are, I have no intention of—"

The voice cut in. "If you care at all what happens to David, be there. And be alone."

There was a click and the line went dead.

Jessica stood unmoving, the receiver still in her hand. She blinked. How utterly absurd! This was the stuff of thousands of bad thrillers: the mysterious message, the lonely rendezvous (an empty warehouse, of course) at night, and that final touch of melodrama, the ominous instructions to come alone. It was really unbelievable.

She put down the receiver. Was it a joke, a student hoax aimed at the visiting mystery writer? She thought not. The voice had been too sincere. A professional actress might have achieved that degree of verisimilitude, but not a student. The question in that case was what was she to do? Notify the police? Tell David? Seek Edmund's advice? Or ignore the whole thing?

Or go?

It would be quite insane, of course, a ridiculous risk. How many times had she read of thriller heroes or heroines going off on perilous nocturnal missions of this kind—and wondered why they were such fools. She had even sent her own heroine once—though in that story had made sure the girl really had no choice.

Jessica certainly had a choice. But for the first time she realized why the protagonist of a mystery story really couldn't be allowed to turn down such an invitation. It was a dare, a challenge. You could never afterward feel quite the same about someone who backed down. And you could never feel quite the same about yourself if *you* backed down. Besides, she had promised to do all she could to help David. Moreover, no one involved in this case could have any possible motive for wanting to kill her.

Could they?

*   *   *

It would be untrue to say that Jessica didn't feel nervous as the taxi weaved its way through the maze of streets leading to the docks of Harbor Island. In fact, she felt very frightened. A dozen times she opened her mouth to tell the cabbie she'd changed her mind and to drive her to police headquarters instead; and a dozen times she closed it. She was about to open it a thirteenth time, when he said: "This is it, lady."

Jessica stared out the window. She could see very little: a high, faint moon being the only illumination. To her left, somewhere, was the ocean; to her right (a mere darker patch against the sky), a large, forbidding building, apparently one of a row of similar ones. Jessica peered toward it dubiously. Then she looked at the luminous dial of her watch. It was two minutes to ten. Quickly, before she had time to change her mind, she opened the door and got out.

"How much?" she asked the driver.

He was looking worried. "Say, lady, you sure you want to be dropped here?"

"I'm quite sure I *don't*. But I've got to be."

"You a cop?"

"No."

"Spy?"

She managed a smile. "No. I just have to meet someone."

"Look, lady, any guy who gets a dame to meet him at a dump like this ain't worth it, believe me."

"Thanks for the warning. But it's nothing like that. And I'm not up to anything illegal, believe me."

"I never figured you was. You got respectable written all over you."

"I hope that's a compliment."

"You want I should wait?"

Jessica thought. It would be very comforting to have this nice little man within reasonable distance. She said, "Could you drive a few hundred yards, park, wait ten minutes and then come back?"

"Sure."

"Thanks. Then do that, will you? Here." She handed

him ten dollars. "Take that for now, and we'll settle up properly later. Drive away now, please."

He shrugged. "You're the boss. But I don't like it." He looked at his watch. "Ten minutes it is."

Jessica stood still, watching the taxi as it drove off. Then she turned and surveyed the vast bulk of the deserted warehouse. Everything was deathly silent. There was no wind tonight, and she couldn't even hear the water. She wished she'd never come. She wished she were back in her hotel. Or, better still, home in Cabot Cove.

She opened her purse, took out a flashlight, and walked toward the warehouse, the sound of her footsteps echoing back to her as she did. Outside the entrance, she stopped and took a deep breath. Then she went inside.

It was now totally dark. Jessica switched on her flashlight and swung it around and up. The cavernous reaches of the building stretched far beyond the range of the beam. Apart from a few piles of empty packing cases, the place seemed quite empty. She shivered, licked her lips and called out, "Hello?"

Her voice seemed to come back at her from all sides, but there was no response. She tried again, slightly louder. "Hello! Anybody here?"

Still the silence was total. Jessica stood, uncertain as to her next move. She wanted very much to leave. She'd done what had been demanded of her. She could be expected to do no more. And there certainly seemed to be nobody here. But, if there was no human being present, there might well be rats. She felt she would almost prefer her flashlight's beam to fall on a masked man with a gun than on the beady red eyes of a rat. Oh dear!

Then she heard a sound. She froze. What was it? Footsteps? Something being dragged? Fighting down a rising panic, Jessica called out again: "Who's there?"

She shone her flashlight around frantically—and nearly screamed out loud as the beam alighted on a human figure.

It was a woman. And she was staggering toward Jessica, dragging her feet. Her face was ashen, her expression ghastly. She seemed for a moment to be wearing a dress with a garish abstract pattern of scarlet patches. Then Jessica saw that the scarlet was blood.

As Jessica took a step toward her, the woman raised one despairing hand; then her knees buckled and she fell forward to the floor.

Momentarily forgetting all possible risk, Jessica ran to her and knelt down. She turned the woman over and shone the light into her face. Then she picked up the woman's limp wrist and groped for her pulse. There was nothing.

Jessica got shakily to her feet and for five seconds stood quite still. Then she turned and ran.

She ran as she had not run in years, out of the warehouse and in the direction taken by the taxi, her flashlight's beam making a crazy, jumping path before her. She prayed the cabbie hadn't changed his mind and gone. She was just beginning to think he had when at last she saw the cab.

She staggered up to the driver's window. He turned a startled face to her as she gasped out, "Get on your radio—quick! There's been a murder!"

For a moment he stared at her. Then without a word he reached for his microphone.

The black-and-white was there in ten minutes, though it seemed an hour. Jessica heard the siren long before she saw the car. She jumped out of the cab where she'd been sitting, breathless and speechless. She stood, waving her arms. The car screeched to a halt in front of her, and two reassuringly large uniformed policemen got out. Jessica hurried up to them, pointing behind her.

"Along there, about two hundred yards. Warehouse thirty-three."

One of the officers stepped back and opened the rear door of the car. "Get in. Show us."

Jessica did as she was told.

Half a minute later, the police car pulled up outside the warehouse and the two officers went inside, Jessica at their heels. Both had drawn their revolvers and one was carrying a powerful flashlight.

For a moment Jessica had a horrible fear that the body would have disappeared. But no: it was still there.

One officer knelt down by it while the other stood, shining his flashlight around. After a few seconds the first one got to his feet. "She's dead, all right." He looked at Jessica. "You know her?"

She nodded. "I've never spoken to her, but I know who she is. Her name is Lila Schroeder. She's the wife of the swimming coach at Sequoia University."

Chapter Six

"IT was a damn fool thing to do, Mrs. Fletcher," Lieutenant Andrews growled.

"I know," Jessica said.

"You should have phoned me as soon as you received the call."

"Yes. But if I had, she might not have been willing to talk."

His face creased into a sudden, unexpected smile. "I certainly give you top marks for guts."

Jessica looked surprised. "Thank you, Lieutenant."

It was an hour later, and they were in his warm, brightly lit office at police headquarters. Jessica had told her story and was now gratefully sipping at a steaming cup of coffee.

Suddenly Andrews was serious again. "Well, she didn't talk, anyway."

"No, she never had a chance."

"This so-called proof she was going to give you, that Tolliver couldn't have killed the Brevard woman—do you have any idea . . . ?"

"None whatsoever. I've told you all I know."

He grunted. "Well, we'll see if he can throw any light on it soon. I've given orders for him to be picked up."

"You don't suspect him of this murder too?"

"Let's just say I want to know where he's been for the last few hours."

Jessica put down her coffee cup. "But, Lieutenant,

wouldn't it be awfully stupid for him to kill off his own alibi?''

"What I'm thinking, ma'am, is that we're dealing with a very clever young man who might have set this whole thing up to make us *think* he had an alibi; and then eliminated the girl before she could say anything—hoping we'd fall into the trap of thinking just as you are.''

Jessica shook her head. "Really, Mr. Andrews, that does seem to be a scheme of quite incredible, almost unbelievable, subtlety.''

He shrugged. "Maybe. We'll see. Now, we'd better do something about getting you back to your hotel.''

Probably as a result of nervous reaction, Jessica slept like a log that night and was late getting up the following morning. She turned the radio on first thing. The murder of Lila Schroeder was the lead item on the local news. It was reported that her husband Jack had been taken in for questioning. The murder weapon had been found about twenty yards from the body: an old longshoreman's hook that might have been on the premises for years. An unpremeditated murder—or a clever attempt to make this seem the case? No mention was made of David—or, Jessica was pleased to note—of her own part in the affair.

Immediately after breakfast she started work. However, she had only just got under way when there came a tap on the door. She gave a sigh and went to answer it.

It was David. He looked terrible—pale, haggard, and red-eyed.

Jessica stood back and let him in. "I didn't expect to see you today,'' she said.

"I told you I'd be here, didn't I?''

"Yes, but I heard last night that the police were going to bring you in for questioning.''

"They did. I was there for hours. Do you mind if I sit down?'' He did so, then looked up at her. "Oh, Jessica, I just can't believe Lila is dead.''

She was amazed to see tears in his eyes. "Were you so very close?'' she asked.

He nodded and his eyes dropped.

"David, she told me on the phone she had proof you couldn't have killed Alison. Was that true?"

"She could have given me an alibi." He looked up at her again. "The night Alison was killed Lila and I were together—the whole night."

"Oh," said Jessica. "I see."

He managed a faint smile. "You don't approve?"

"She was a married woman, David."

"In name only." He got to his feet. "She and Jack had been living apart for months. She wanted a divorce. He drove her to it with his insane jealousy. She only had to smile at a man and he'd accuse her of having an affair. And he'd go crazy with rage. He threatened to kill her a dozen times. She had to leave him."

"It seems his jealousy might have been justified."

"No!" He shook his head sharply. "There was nothing between Lila and me until after her marriage had broken up."

"But had her marriage broken up—finally?"

"As far as she was concerned, yes. Jack, of course, had been hounding her to go back to him, but there was no way she would have."

"If she could have given you an alibi, why didn't she?"

"I wouldn't let her. Jack would have had to find out about it. And I was scared what he'd do if he discovered she'd been with me that night."

"Scared what he'd do to her? Or to you, David?"

"To her, of course. He just wouldn't accept they were through. He said if he couldn't have her, nobody would. He meant it; she believed it. Why else would she choose to meet you down at that damn warehouse?"

He suddenly put his head in his hands and gave a groan. "Oh, why did she have to do it? I warned her not to."

"Why did she do it?"

He stared. "To clear me. She felt she couldn't go on any longer—"

"No, I mean why *me*?"

"Oh, she was at your lecture the other night. I guess it

was the first lecture she'd ever been to. And she was bowled over by your brain-power. She was convinced that if she put the whole story to you, you'd think up a way to solve everything."

He gave a twisted grin. "Poor little Lila. She was the sweetest person you could imagine. But in some ways she was really incredibly dumb."

On the last word David's voice broke and he turned away for a moment. Then he looked back at Jessica. "I'm sorry. I didn't mean that like it sounded."

"I know what you meant," Jessica said softly.

David brushed a hand quickly across his eyes. "Well," he said briskly, "better get to work."

"David, how much sleep have you had?"

"Oh, not a lot."

"Any?"

"Well, I guess not, now you come to mention it."

"Then you hurry straight home and go to bed."

"Oh, I couldn't—"

"You could and you will. Now scoot. I have no work for you today, anyway."

"Well, if you're sure . . ."

"Be here early tomorrow."

When he'd gone, Jessica went on to the patio and stared out over the city. In the distance, through mist and fog, she could make out the Space Needle. Slender, solitary, and a little spooky.

Jessica sighed. Much against her will, she was being inexorably drawn into this case. It was a nuisance. But she remembered the decision she'd reached at the end of the Lydecker case: that if such events came her way again, she wouldn't fight, but rather use her gifts in any way that seemed necessary. And her book was near enough finished for her to take a break from it today.

She sat down, got out a notebook and spent ten minutes writing in it. Then she rose and put on her hat and coat. She needed some information, and probably the best person to supply it was Edmund.

* * *

Jessica tapped on the door leading to Edmund's office. Amelia Browne's voice called, "Come in," and Jessica opened the door.

Amelia looked up from her typewriter in the anteroom. There was the beginning of a smile on her face. But it froze ever so slightly at the sight of Jessica.

"Oh, good morning, Mrs. Fletcher."

"Good morning, Amelia. How are you?"

"Very well. I'm afraid Dr. Gerard isn't in just now."

"Oh. Do you know when he will be?"

"I really couldn't say." Her manner was decidedly cold.

"Well, it's rather important I see him. Do you mind if I wait?"

"If you wish." She indicated a chair, then turned away and started typing quickly. Jessica sat down.

Five minutes passed. Then, when Amelia stopped typing to change the paper, Jessica said suddenly, "Amelia, despite what you think, I am not a rival."

Amelia's head jerked up. "I—I beg your pardon?"

"Edmund and I are dear friends and nothing more, believe me."

Amelia's face slowly went red. "Mrs. Fletcher," she said, "you misjudge me, really—"

Jessica spoke impatiently. "Oh, Amelia, for heaven's sake, only a blind person could misread your feelings for Edmund. I think he must be in desperate need of a good optometrist."

She smiled, and suddenly, a little awkwardly, Amelia smiled too.

"That's better," Jessica said. "Now please, let me be your ally, because I'm certainly not your enemy.

"I wasn't aware my feelings were so transparent. I was very fond of Mrs. Gerard, I really was, and she was good for him. Then when she died . . ." She broke off and shrugged. "If patience is a virtue, I'm the most virtuous of women."

"All he needs is some gentle nudging," Jessica told her. "Not from me. From you."

"I'm working up to it."

At that moment the door opened and Edmund came in. She stood up. "Hello, Edmund."

"Hello, Jessica. I didn't expect to see you today."

"Can you spare me a few minutes?"

"Of course. Come on through."

He took her into his private office and they sat down. She wasted no time. "Have you heard about Lila Schroeder?"

His face clouded. "Yes—on the radio. And Jack Schroeder taken in. Terrible—terrible."

"Did you know that I was the one to find her?"

"No." He stared. "Good Lord!"

She told him the story of the previous night. When she'd finished, he shook his head in disbelief. "My word, Jess, what a risk you took! If she was alive when you got there, it means the murderer was almost certainly still nearby."

"I know. But I didn't come here to talk about my own exploits. Edmund, you said *the murderer*. Does that mean you don't think it's her husband?"

He shook his head helplessly. "I just don't know. I can't really believe it of him."

"Is it true he was insanely jealous?"

"Jealous, yes. I don't know about *insanely*. But, of course, Lila was a very beautiful young woman. It's natural, I suppose, he should think other men were after her."

"Does he have a temper?"

He paused for a moment. "Yes, he does."

"Violent?"

"He's been involved in fights. I don't think he'd use violence against a woman. Lila certainly never complained of that; their fights were purely verbal affairs, I believe. But, of course, I don't really know. You say the police had David Tolliver in for questioning, too?"

"Yes."

"It's beginning to look black for him, Jess—two women he knew, both murdered."

"The other night at dinner, you were arguing against his being a killer."

"I know, but one has to face facts. And, of course, as I explained, I don't know him well. I'm beginning to fear I was wrong about him."

"But Lila told me she could prove him innocent of Alison's murder."

"So you said." He looked thoughtful. "I wonder how. Were she and Alison friends, perhaps? Did Alison tell Lila about some *other* man she was afraid of? And then did Lila see them together, or something like that?"

"Oh no," Jessica said. "I should have explained; David came to me this morning. Lila was going to give him an alibi. They were together all through the night Alison was murdered."

Edmund stared. "Lila said that?"

"She was going to, according to David."

He shook his head. "I'm sorry, Jess. I can't swallow it."

"Why?"

"Well, isn't it very convenient for him that she should say that just before dying? Suppose he forced her to call you and say what she did—and then killed her before she could recant?"

Jessica sighed. "You're as bad as Lieutenant Andrews. But I just don't believe it. If she'd called the *police* and said what she'd said to me, I might credit it. But I'd still have great difficulty in believing David could hit Alison over the head with a statuette, or kill Lila with a long-shoreman's hook. I'm *certain* he's not a violent type."

Edmund smiled. "Well, you're the expert."

"I'm no expert. I just have feelings. And that's a very strong one. But, Edmund, it doesn't have to have been either Jack or David, does it?"

"Of course not."

"In fact—and this is what I principally wanted to ask you about—I do have an idea about someone else who might have had a motive."

"Who's that?"

She didn't answer directly. "Lila was at my first lecture, remember?"

"Yes, it was rather surprising."

"I don't think she really came to hear me. I think she wanted to see Todd Lowery."

Edmund eyed her sharply. "What makes you think that?"

"The way she was looking at him. The way she followed him out. And he didn't like it. He did his best to avoid her. But she wasn't having any."

Edmund was looking at her with admiration. "You're remarkable, Jess, you really are. Well, it's true—and please, this is between you and me: Lila did have a brief affair with Todd. But it's over."

"Are you quite certain it's over?"

"I couldn't swear it on oath, but I believe so."

"Who ended it?"

"He did."

"Suppose Lila didn't want to end it? Suppose she was in love with him, wanted to marry him, and was threatening to tell his wife?"

"You're suggesting Todd would kill her to stop her? No, Jess, I find that hard to believe. Besides, there's absolutely nothing that I know of to link Todd with Alison Brevard."

"Of course not. But, Edmund, there doesn't have to have been any connection between the two murders. Lila needn't have been killed because of anything she was going to tell me about the Brevard case."

He pursed his lips. "Bit of a coincidence, otherwise, isn't it?"

"Yes. But coincidences do happen. Or somebody might be using the first murder as a sort of smoke screen for the second."

"I suppose that's possible. But, Jess, you're wrong on one point: there *is* a known connection between the two cases."

"What's that?"

"David Tolliver."

*   *   *

Jack Schroeder was released by the police for lack of evidence at noon that day. That development was reported on the lunchtime news, and at two o'clock that afternoon Jessica was ringing the front door bell of the neat suburban home which, until a few months ago, Schroeder had shared with his wife. There was no reply, and after about fifteen seconds she rang again. A voice from inside called roughly: "If that's another reporter, you can clear off. I got nothing to say."

"It's not," Jessica called back.

There was a pause, then the door was yanked open.

"Well?" Jack Schroeder said.

He was a tall, lean, lithe man with the well-developed shoulders of the athlete. His dark hair, brushed back, was receding slightly and his face was thin, almost gaunt. He was in need of a shave.

"I'm Jessica Fletcher," she said.

"Oh, the murder lady. What d'you want?"

"You may have heard that it was I who found your wife. Immediately after the—the attack."

"So?"

"Well, I just wanted you to know that she didn't suffer for any length of time. One second she was on her feet; the next she'd collapsed. She died almost instantly."

"Well, thanks for telling me. Is that all?"

"Mr. Schroeder, can I speak to you privately for a few minutes?"

"What about?"

"About your wife."

"Look, if you're thinking of ripping off Lila's death for your next book, forget it. She's dead. Let her rest in peace."

"I have no intention of writing about her. I *am* interested in who killed her. I thought you might be, too."

"How d'you know it wasn't me?"

"I don't."

"Taking a bit of a risk, then, aren't you?"

"You wouldn't be such a fool as to kill me here and

now, in your own home, in broad daylight. Besides, I have nothing, er, on you that might give you a motive."

"Ah, but I got an uncontrollable temper, don't I? Or so the cops say."

"I shall do nothing to provoke it."

He hesitated, then said, "Oh, you might as well come in, I suppose."

He turned and went back into the house, leaving Jessica to follow him in and close the front door.

The living room in which she found herself had obviously not been cleaned for a week. Empty coffee mugs and beer cans were dotted about; items of clothing were on every chair; and the place smelled stale. She ached to get busy with a Hoover, duster and polish, but there were more important matters on hand.

"You probably think I'm just being nosy," she said.

"Aren't you?"

"No. I tried not to get involved. Your wife involved me herself. It seems there's no firm evidence—forensic-type evidence—as to who might have killed her. Which could mean the case will never be solved. And unsolved murders are bad for everybody involved—particularly the surviving spouse. A shadow of suspicion always lurks over them. Now, of course, it may be you did kill her and don't want the truth to come out. But if you didn't, it would be advisable to talk with me. If we put our heads together, we just might get somewhere."

He stared at her for a moment. Then he grunted. "Better sit down."

He indicated a chair by snatching a dirty shirt off it. He tossed the shirt into a corner. Jessica sat. He pulled out an upright chair from the table, swung it around and sat astride it, his hands resting on the back.

"Could be I'm talking because I want you to *think* I'm innocent."

"Of course," she replied.

"What did you want to ask?"

"Did you threaten to kill Lila?"

"I guess so. I also threatened to win an Olympic gold

twelve years back. I didn't even make the team. I'm real bad at follow-through."

"You know, Mr. Schroeder, if this was your manner at the police station, you can't have done yourself much good. Why so flip, so apparently callous? I believe you loved your wife very much."

There was a momentary hesitation, a sudden look in his eyes, and Jessica knew she'd hit a nerve. Then the look was gone and he was saying: "So did a lot of other guys."

"Naturally. But did she love them?"

"Depends what you mean by love."

"You're saying she was just a tramp."

"No!"

The word came out like a gunshot. He got suddenly to his feet, nearly knocking the chair over. He turned away, groping for words, then spun around to face her again.

"It may have seemed like that. It did to me at one time. But I figured it out. The problem was, she could never get enough love. She craved affection, a sense of being wanted. Maybe it was something she missed as a kid. All I know is that I wasn't enough for her."

"And you found that hard to take?"

"Sure I did. Wouldn't anybody?"

"Only if he loved his wife. If he didn't, he'd just get a divorce and start over."

"Okay—so I loved her." He said it defiantly, as though he was admitting something shameful.

Jessica changed tack. "You know she called me, saying she could clear David Tolliver of suspicion of Alison Brevard's murder?"

He stared. "No. I didn't know that."

"He claims she was going to give him an alibi for that whole night."

"Bull!"

Jessica raised her eyebrows. "Are you saying they weren't lovers? Wasn't he one of the men you were jealous of?"

"Jealous of Pretty-Boy? No way. Lila knew him. But that's all. He'd have been too young for her. She liked men a few years older than herself."

"Such as Professor Lowery?"

There was silence. Jack looked away. "At one time."

"But not currently?"

He turned back. "Mrs. Fletcher, I don't know. Lila and I were living apart. I have a job. I couldn't follow her around. I couldn't afford a private detective. So I just don't know who she'd been seeing. And that's what I told the police. If I had any clue about her present lover, do you think I wouldn't say?"

"No; obviously you would." Jessica stood up. "So there's nothing else you can tell me?"

He shook his head. "Except that I didn't do it."

"I see. Well, thank you for your time, Mr. Schroeder. I'm sorry to have—"

He interrupted. "Maybe there's one thing."

"What's that?"

"The cops told me—asked if I could explain something. I couldn't. They found her purse behind one of those crates. There was a thousand dollars in an envelope inside it. She didn't draw it from the bank, and there was nothing she could have sold to raise it. Somebody must have given it to her. But they don't know who. Or why."

Chapter Seven

"I THOUGHT that for my final lecture," Jessica said, "I would look at the technique of *writing* detective stories—the particular problems which face the mystery author. And there are problems which are unique to this genre, which give it, for the author, both a fascination and a frustration all its own.

"For example, a so-called straight novelist can write one chapter about character A, a second about character B, and so on. The author doesn't normally have to concern himself with what B is doing at precisely the same moment that A is having the adventures in chapter one. The mystery writer, on the other hand, frequently has to consider not only the movements of B at this same time, but also those of C, D and perhaps half a dozen others. They all have to be worked into an extremely intricate pattern, sometimes before you even put pen to paper. And the reason, of course, is that it must be possible for a number of different characters to have committed the crime. It's no good finding yourself in a situation where at the time of the second murder, one of your potential suspects is lecturing at a university and several of the others are in the audience—thereby leaving only one person without an alibi. And, therefore, the guilty party.

"It's necessary, in fact, for the author to put himself—or herself—into the mind of the murderer. Let's take a specific but imaginary crime. A young woman is unhappily married to a jealous and perhaps violent husband. She needs love and affection. He cannot provide them. A perfect recipe for the murder of passion. The young woman is found dead. The suspects are legion.''

Jessica stepped down from the rostrum and stood immediately in front of the first row of spectators.

"Now, what's our first problem?"

She let her eyes run along the row of students. One said, "Check out the alibis."

Jessica shook her head. "Not exactly. That's thinking like a detective: an admirable exercise sometimes. But in this case we're not *solving* a murder. We're setting it up. So again: what's our problem?"

A familiar voice said, "*Create* the alibis."

It was David. He was sitting relaxed and easy in his seat three rows back.

Again Jessica shook her head. "Closer, but still not quite correct. Writers can fairly easily create alibis for their characters: A is lunching with a bishop, B playing golf with a Supreme Court justice, C being interviewed on television, and so on. But that's too easy. As I was trying to indicate, if the writer is to baffle his readers, he must put himself in the shoes of the murderer—who has to *take advantage of non-alibis*. He must time the killing for maximum effectiveness. He chooses . . . a weekday. Evening. Say ten o'clock. He knows A *will* have an alibi. But B won't. C will—but won't be able to reveal it, for fear of letting somebody else down. D's alibi will be provided by, let's say, his mother—so will be worthless.''

Jessica had continued to walk slowly along the row and now came face-to-face with Todd Lowery.

"Who's the obvious suspect in this case?" she asked.

She looked at the professor, almost forcing him to answer.

"The husband, naturally," he said.

"Why?"

He grinned. "Because you haven't yet identified A,B,C or D.''

There was laughter in the room, in which Jessica joined.

"Fair enough," she said, "then let's identify them. Take A—"

David called out: "Don't bother with him—he's got an alibi." There was more laughter.

"Then we'll make it . . . let's see . . . D," Jessica said. "D is a youngish professional man. He's in love, or has been in love, with the victim. But he has a major problem: he's married. Now, do you suppose his wife knows about his relationship with the victim?"

Again she looked at Lowery.

He gazed at her coolly. "I'd say no."

"Good. Because if she *did* know, we'd have to add her name to the list of suspects, and we wouldn't want to do that, would we, Professor?"

"It's your scenario, Mrs. Fletcher."

"Oh, come, come, Professor, this is give-and-take. Tell me about his alibi for the time of the woman's death. Remember that D had the alibi that was worthless."

"I suppose he could have been with his wife."

"And would she swear to that?"

"Yes."

"I suppose now we say this character is B—who, remember, didn't have an alibi at all: he was out somewhere— and alone. Will his wife give him a false alibi—will she *lie* for him?"

Lowery shifted in his seat. "I don't know."

"Do make a guess, Professor. Come on—would she lie for him?"

"She might."

Jessica nodded. "Yes, of course, that is the most any murderer can ever say. The writer, on the contrary, is omniscient, and knows exactly what everybody is going to do and say. Which is why authorship is a much more pleasant activity than homicide can ever be."

She moved on from Lowery and addressed the room at large.

"Now let's turn to another of the author's problems: the search for original motives . . ."

* * *

At the close of the lecture, as the applause broke out, Todd Lowery got hurriedly to his feet and, without a backward glance toward Jessica, walked to the door and went out. She eyed him for a moment thoughtfully, then the students were around her again. There were half a dozen in the front who had attended all the lectures and were full of questions. They begged her to come and have coffee with them, and she hadn't the heart to refuse.

Just then Edmund touched her shoulder. She turned.

"Jess," he said, "I have to see somebody in my office now. Could you come along when these young savages release you? I'd like to talk."

She smiled. "Of course."

"Good. Must rush." He hurried off.

There were some more books to autograph, and the students who had invited her to coffee moved in a clump to one side while she did the signings. When she'd finished, she looked up and saw David standing a few feet away, smiling.

"Hello, David," she said. "You coming for coffee?"

He moved a little closer. "No, thanks. I'm not one for entering into undergraduate discussion groups. I prefer to talk to you on your own. Look, I have a bit of time to spare. I thought I'd go to the hotel and do some more typing. Would you mind?"

"Not at all."

"Oh, I thought, after what you said, that perhaps you wouldn't want me there on my own."

"By no means. As long as you arrange it with me in advance."

He grinned. "Fine. See you later, then."

He stuck his hands in his pockets and strolled out.

The students were bright, keen and extremely knowledgeable, and within a very few minutes Jessica found herself completely involved in an animated discussion on crime fiction. So involved that when she happened to glance at her watch, she was amazed to find she'd been with them for nearly an hour and a half. She speedily said her goodbyes and thanks and left them.

She hurried along to Edmund's office. As she walked up to the door, it opened and he came out. He looked relieved to see her.

"Ah, Jess, good."

"Sorry, Edmund, I got caught up with those students. Have I kept you waiting?"

"It's all right, I had some dictating to do. But I'm afraid I have to dash now. Another meeting. And I did want a serious talk with you. Jess, what are your plans? I suppose, now the lectures are over you'll be leaving Seattle for Kentucky tomorrow?"

"No, actually I thought I'd stay on till I've at least finished the book. I'm quite settled at the hotel now, and I don't want another disruption of my routine until the manuscript's been mailed to my editor. I can go to Abby's anytime. So I'll be around for a few more days."

"Oh, I *am* glad." He sounded genuinely pleased. "Look, can we get together again tomorrow night? We've seen so little of each other, really—just the one dinner and a few fleeting conversations."

"Yes, tomorrow evening will be lovely."

"That's fine. Would you like to go to the same restaurant, or try another one?"

She smiled. "Well, do you know what I'd really like? A home-cooked dinner. I always get the urge after about a week of restaurant and hotel food."

He looked dismayed. "Oh dear, I'm afraid I can't manage that."

"No, but I can. Tell me, Edmund, how long since *you* had a home-cooked dinner?"

"Oh, I don't know. I get invited to somebody's house now and again, but I don't often go."

"Then suppose I cook at your place tomorrow?"

His eyes widened. "Would you really like to do that?"

"I'd love to. I enjoy cooking."

He smiled delightedly. "Well, if you're really sure, that

75

would be wonderful. It'll make the things I want to say to you very much easier, too, than in a restaurant.''

He glanced at his watch. "Oh, Lord, I really must fly." He pulled the office door closed behind him. "I'll call you tomorrow at your hotel, Jess. All right?"

"Right, Edmund. Good night."

"Night, Jess." He hurried away down the corridor, turning to say over his shoulder: "There are no groceries at the house.''

"Leave all that to me.''

He waved a hand and was gone.

When Jessica got back to her hotel room, she expected to find David typing. But in fact there was no sign of him. Then she spotted a note propped up on the typewriter. It read: *Jessica—I had to go out. Sorry. You had a call from Prof. Lowery. Wants you to meet him at his office at nine this evening. Says it's urgent and confidential. Regards, David.*

Jessica slowly lowered the paper. This was most interesting. Her little verbal duel with Lowery must have had some effect. She wondered what he wanted to say. Would he be very angry? Well, she'd soon find out.

No doubt Edmund would be extremely cross if he knew she was going to another nocturnal rendezvous. But visiting the university was quite different from going to a deserted dockside warehouse: there would be people about. And Lowery, if he was guilty, would certainly not be such a fool as to do her harm in his own office, especially after having phoned and passed on a message through a third person.

Of course, there was the trip back to the university. But this time she would take a cab.

The taxi drew up outside the building which housed the English department, and Jessica got out. She looked up. There plainly weren't many people around, but half a dozen windows were lighted. She paid off the driver and made her way inside. Two students passed her and went out, laughing together. Then, apart from her, the big entrance hall was empty. She consulted a wall directory and found that Lowery's office was on the third floor. She crossed to the elevator and pressed the button. Nothing happened. Impatiently she jabbed at it again. Still, there was no response.

Jessica groaned inwardly. Either it was out of order or the power was turned off at night. Probably the latter. She walked resignedly to the stairs and started to climb.

She reached the second-floor landing and paused. It was quite deserted up here and very quiet. Suddenly she felt nervous. She hesitated, then reached into her purse and took out a small cylinder of Mace. She was probably being ridiculously nervous, but it wouldn't do any harm to be on the safe side. Clutching the cylinder in her hand, she walked to the next flight of stairs. Her heels were loud on the marble floor, and the sound echoed back from the high ceilings.

Jessica arrived on the third floor and again paused, both to get her breath and to peer at a couple of nearby door numbers and try to discover which was the way to Lowery's office.

Then from somewhere, from nowhere, a shapeless black figure suddenly materialized at her side. She started to swing around, but at the same instant she was shoved violently in the chest. She had no hope of saving herself, and fell back—straight down the stairs.

The world spun crazily. Lights shot like rockets across her field of vision. She heard herself giving an utterly involuntary scream. For what seemed an age she was conscious of no pain—only a mad whirl of movement. Then she felt an agonizing blow on the front of her head and everything went black.

Chapter Eight

"**Y**OU'RE a very lucky woman, Mrs. Fletcher," the doctor said. "The X rays show nothing's been broken, and the wound to the head is quite superficial."

"Does that mean I can go?" she asked hopefully.

He shook his head firmly. "You've had a nasty fall and been badly shaken. I'm keeping you in overnight for observation."

Jessica sighed and lay back on the pillows. "Well," she said, with a slight smile, "perhaps I'm not altogether sorry. I could use a rest, and it will give me a chance to think."

"Good." Then he looked a trifle embarrassed. "Incidentally, the paramedic who brought you in says that when you came to in the ambulance, you murmured something about being pushed. Is that right?"

She opened her mouth to speak, then thought better of what she'd been going to say. She paused. Then: "If that's what he says, I'm sure he's right. But I must have been delirious. I just fell."

He gave a satisfied nod. "That's what I thought. Now, is there anybody you'd like notified?"

"No; I'd rather not have any visitors."

"Right, then I'll leave you. That was a sedative I gave you just now. It'll start to take effect any moment. You should get a good night's sleep." He crossed to the door.

"Thank you, doctor. Good night."

"Good night."

He went out, switching out the light. Jessica lay with her eyes closed. *Lucky*, he had said; he didn't know how lucky. That had been a deliberate attempt on her life. Not that there would have been any point in telling him, or in reporting it to the police. She couldn't give them the slightest clue as to the identity of the man who had done it. And it might be better to keep him in suspense about how much she knew or suspected.

But who had it been? Lowery was the obvious suspect. Too obvious? Or would he rely on her thinking that? Was he pulling a sophisticated double bluff? It was just the sort of thing that might appeal to an academic who was also a mystery buff. Or was she fooling herself, avoiding the only logical answer as to the identity of her attacker: the only other person who knew she was going to be at the English building . . . ?

But why? Why should he want . . . ? What harm could she do . . . ?

Jessica slept.

It was half past two the following afternoon when Jessica again ascended to the third floor of the English building. This time, however, she took the elevator.

She located the office of Todd Lowery and tapped on the door. A voice called loudly: "Come in."

She entered. Lowery was alone in the office, working at a big desk that was covered by papers. He looked surprised to see her (just surprised, she noted; not guilty or shocked), and got to his feet.

"Mrs. Fletcher! I say, what have you been doing to yourself?"

Jessica fingered the bandage on her head. "Oh, hadn't you heard, professor? I had a fall."

"Not too bad, I hope."

"Bad enough. I was in the hospital overnight."

"Really? Where did it happen? Oh, please sit down."

"Here." Jessica sat.

"Here?"

"In this building. I fell down the stairs from this floor to the second. I'm told that a research student, working late, heard me and called an ambulance. I was on my way to keep our appointment. I expect you wondered why I didn't show up.''

He looked blank. "Our appointment?''

Jessica stared. "Are you saying you *didn't* call and leave a message asking me to meet you here at nine last night—on an urgent and confidential matter?''

It was his turn to stare. "I most certainly did not.''

"I see.'' Jessica looked at him thoughtfully.

"What sort of urgent and confidential things could I have to speak to you about last night?''

"That's what I was wondering. I imagined . . . Lila. Professor Lowery, I said I fell down the stairs. Actually, I was pushed.''

"My God! Are you sure?''

"Quite sure.''

"Have you reported—'' He broke off. Suddenly he'd gone pale. "Mrs. Fletcher, I hope you're not thinking that I—I lured you here to—to attempt . . .'' Again he left the sentence unfinished.

"Well, it certainly would have been extremely foolish.'' She paused. "Or extremely ingenious.''

"Mrs. Fletcher, I give you my word: I was at home all yesterday evening. As it happens, I made no calls at all. My wife can vouch—''

He stopped short, then gave a slow and rather feeble smile. "Of course—the worthless alibi. And I may as well admit right now that the same thing applies to the time of Lila's murder. My wife and I went straight home from the reception and stayed there—alone.''

"I haven't accused you of murdering Lila, Professor.''

"No . . . but you think I might have pushed you downstairs, don't you? But I ask you, what reason could I possibly have?''

"I don't know. Except that I realize you *were* quite angry with me yesterday, after the lecture.''

"I admit it. I was.''

"I feel rather embarrassed about that now, to tell you the truth."

"Don't be. Your little charade knocked some sense into me. I realized how ridiculous I'd been. My wife and I were up all night, talking. She's a very understanding woman. She believed me when I told her my fling with Lila was over a couple of months ago. To my great relief, as a matter of fact. Anyway, Emily and I are going away for a week, just the two of us, to try to put it back together. So, I have no cause to wish you harm. You can see that, can't you?"

Jessica nodded. "Yes. I can see that." She did not add, as it was on her mind to: "I can see you have no cause to wish me harm—*now*."

After leaving Lowery, Jessica want back to her hotel. She found she was still quite shaky on her feet. She lay down on her bed for an hour, and at the end of that time felt much better. She was just about to call Room Service for some tea when there was a knock from the corridor. She put down the phone and opened the door. It was Edmund. He looked immensely relieved to see her.

"Jessica, are you all right?"

"Fine, Edmund, thank you."

"I've been trying to reach you all day. I called the hospital early, as soon as I heard about your accident from the research student who found you; but you were still sleeping. I called again later and they said you'd been discharged. Immediately after lunch I phoned here and they told me you'd gone out. Then I ran into Lowery on campus, and he told me about your visit to him. Jess, he says you claimed you were pushed down those stairs. Is that true?"

"Yes, Edmund, quite true."

"Great Scot!" He'd gone pale. "What's this place coming to?"

"Sit down and I'll tell you about it."

She returned to the phone, ordered tea for two, and then narrated the whole story of the previous evening.

When she'd finished, he shook his head incredulously.
"I feel responsbile," he said slowly. "If I'd never invited
you here . . ."

"Oh, that's foolish, Edmund. How could you possibly
know what was going to happen? Besides, I wasn't seriously hurt, and by tomorrow—apart from a few minor
bruises—I should be quite all right."

"Well, thank heaven for that. Jess . . . you don't really
suspect Todd Lowery, do you?"

She spread her hands helplessly. "I honestly don't know.
He could have done it. He could have killed Lila—to
prevent his wife and the university from finding out about
their affair. On the other hand, his wife seems to have
taken the news of the affair very well; and *you* knew
about it anyway. In addition, I have to admit there isn't a
shred of hard evidence against him."

"My dear," he said quietly, "you know who it has to
have been, don't you? David Tolliver."

"But *why*?" She got to her feet and took two or three
indecisive steps around the room.

"I don't know," he said. "But I believe he killed the
Brevard woman. And I also believe he bribed Lila to
supply him with a false alibi that night. Then he got cold
feet—realized that if she had second thoughts and reported
the bribe to the police, he'd almost certainly find himself
under arrest for the murder of Alison. Perhaps Lila was
already getting attacks of conscience and was threatening
to back down. So he killed her before she could, but not
before she'd told you she could prove him innocent."

"But, Edmund, that still doesn't explain why he should
attack *me*!"

"I can only assume he's frightened of you. He knows of
your reputation as an amateur detective and that you're
interested in this case. It's quite possible that during all the
conversations you've had with him, he's given himself
away—slipped up by saying something that implicates him
in the Brevard murder."

Jessica shook her head firmly. "He hasn't. I'm sure of
it."

"Then he *thinks* he has. And he's terrified that you're suddenly going to put two and two together. Jess, when a killer who's murdered twice believes his security is threatened in any way, he'll kill again at the drop of a hat."

"I know, I know. I just can't picture David as a killer. Not of that type, anyway. He may be weak. He may be unscrupulous where money or women are concerned. But after a lifetime's study of human nature, I'd stake a lot of my belief that he's not capable of violence. And remember there's no hard evidence against him, either. He hasn't been caught out in any lies about his movements—"

Edmund interrupted. "He has." His voice was harsh.

Jessica stared. "But the police have questioned him at length—"

"I don't mean by the police. But he claimed Lila was with him the night Alison was killed."

"You don't *know* that wasn't true."

"I do. You see"—he took a deep breath—"that night Lila was with *me*."

There was a long silence. Then Jessica said softly, "I see." She sat down slowly.

"You don't seem surprised. You hadn't guessed?"

She looked at him. "No. I hadn't. I didn't think that. But it was at the back of my mind that you knew Lila better than anyone thought. You said something about her never complaining that her husband used violence against her. It seemed strange. She'd hardly complain to you about that—not unless you were quite close friends."

"I'd like to explain about—" he started.

Just then there was a tap on the door. It was a waiter with the tea things. When he'd gone and Jessica was pouring the tea, she said, "Edmund, there's no call for you to explain anything. Whatever went on between you and Lila is your business, not mine."

"Jess, nothing went on. Not really. Please, I'd like to tell you."

"Very well." She handed him a cup of tea. He took it, but didn't drink."

"Several months ago, Lila came to me to ask if there was any work for her at the university. I think really she was just bored. Well, she wasn't exactly the academic type, but I happened to know that Todd Lowery was looking for someone to help with the indexing of a book he's nearly finished on Jacobean poetry, and I put them in touch. That's how their affair started.

"The first I knew about it was a month or two later, when Lila came and told me. She was in an awful state. She was terrified of her husband. He suspected what was going on and had threatened to kill her. Also, she was full of guilt about possibly breaking up Todd and Emily's marriage. She was still in love with him, but didn't know what to do. You know the sort of thing."

Jessica nodded.

"Well, I talked to her like a Dutch uncle. I told her she should give Todd up, make a clean break, and so on. Nothing very original or wise. To make a long story short, she did break with Todd. Unfortunately, though, that didn't improve things with Jack. He didn't believe the affair was over. She continued to come and see me, pouring out her troubles. At last I began to take Todd's place in her affections. Though I really believe I was always more of a father figure to her than anything else. I admit I was attracted to her. I was lonely, she was young and very pretty. It happens."

"Edmund," said Jessica, "honestly, there's no need—"

He raised a hand. "Please, Jess, let me finish. The upshot of it was that we started going out together. There was never anything more to it than that. All the same, she *was* married to one of the university employees, and I did feel guilty about it. I used to take her way out of town, to a little place called the Lumberjack Inn. Nevertheless, we both felt terribly furtive about it. I kept imagining somebody seeing us there and telling Jack—being cited in their divorce. The works."

He gave a wry grin. "I got so neurotic, I remember that after the first few times I even stopped paying the bill by credit card—just to make it harder for anybody to prove I'd been there. It was all very stupid.''

He stopped and sipped at his tea. Jessica just waited. At last he looked up and continued. "However, I've gotten away from the main point. Which is that on the night Alison Brevard was killed, Lila and I were at the Lumberjack Inn until past midnight. We didn't get back to Seattle until nearly twelve forty-five in the morning. So you see, when Tolliver said Lila could give him an alibi for the night of Alison's death, he was lying.''

Jessica didn't speak for several moments. She drank some tea, then put her cup down before asking, "Are you certain you haven't mistaken the date?''

"Quite certain. It was the last time we went to the Lumberjack. And it was the night Lila believed someone had followed her home and tried to run her down. I called her—''

"Tell me about that.''

"Lila was sure this car was following us when we were on our way back. She was terrified it was Jack. I told her the driver just happened to be going to Seattle by the same route as we. Anyway, I dropped her in town and put her in a taxi; I never took her all the way home, of course—just in case. When I called her the next day, she told me she was sure the same car had tailed the cab to her address. Then when she got out and was crossing the road, it came roaring up and very nearly knocked her down. She had to run for the sidewalk. She said to me on the phone that there were very nearly *two* women murdered in Seattle the previous night. So, you see, I couldn't have mistaken the date.''

"You've never mentioned this before, Edmund.''

He hesitated. "No. I'd more or less forgotten it. I assumed it was just a drunk driver who'd nearly run her down, and that she'd imagined the part about being tailed. Are you saying there's a connection between that and her murder?''

Jessica shrugged. "Who knows? The fact remains, she

has been murdered since. I suppose she didn't get the car's license number?''

"I'm sure she didn't. She would have said."

"Or a description?"

"She just said a car."

"You didn't see it?"

"I just saw the lights of *a* car in my rearview mirror. I'm not even sure it was the same car all the time. Lila kept looking back, and swore it was."

"Who else knew you were at this Lumberjack Inn with Lila that night?"

"Nobody, as far as I'm concerned. And I'm sure she didn't tell anybody, in case it got back to her husband. Jess, I don't think there's anything in this."

"Don't you? Well, I think one can be pretty sure when an attempt's been made on one's life. It's a sort of gut certainty." She smiled. "And I should know."

"Maybe you're right. But in Lila's case it would be impossible to prove it—after all this time."

"Oh, I know. But if it's true, it proves something else, doesn't it? That at least half of your suspicions of David are unfounded."

He frowned. "I don't see that."

"It would mean that there must have been *two* murderers around that night. The one who killed Alison couldn't at the same time have been following you and Lila from the inn and attempting to run her down. So, even if David was one of them, he couldn't have killed both women, as you suspected."

"Oh, I see. Unless, of course, somebody else entirely tried to kill Lila *that* night, which is stretching coincidence too far, I agree. No, I don't believe there *was* a deliberate attempt to run her down. Jess, I told you this story— although it makes me look very foolish—because it serves one useful purpose: it exposes David Tolliver as the liar— and killer—he is."

Jessica looked at him. "You're very sure, aren't you, Edmund?"

"Yes; and if we were talking about anybody but him, you would be, too."

Jessica sighed and stood up. She shook her head slowly. "I don't know. Maybe you're right, Edmund, maybe you're right."

"I'm sure I am." He too stood up. "Anyway, I must go. I've said what I came to say. Oh, about tonight—"

"Do you mind if we postpone it until tomorrow, Edmund? I think I'd enjoy it more then. I'd probably cook better, too."

"Yes, of course, that'll be fine. Get some rest now. I'll call you tomorrow."

"Yes, do that."

He said goodbye and went out. Jessica sat down again. She really did feel terribly tired. The hours of work on the book, the added mental strain of the lectures, and now this fall, had all combined to exhaust her. At the moment she was aching all over. Probably the best thing she could do was go to bed.

There was a tap on the door. The waiter for the tea things, she thought. She hadn't bolted the door after Edmund had left, so she called: "Come in."

The door opened and David entered.

He grinned. "Hi."

Jessica stared at him. She got slowly to her feet. "David, what are you doing here?"

His eyebrows went up. "I work for you, don't I?"

"I never expected to see you again."

"Why?"

"After the lie you told me."

"What do you mean? I never told you any lie."

"You told me Lila could give you an alibi for Alison's murder. That wasn't true. I know who *was* with Lila at that time. It wasn't you."

He'd gone pale. He said: "Oh, Lord . . ."

"Why, David? Why?"

He ran his fingers through his hair. "Why do you think? I'm in a jam, Jessica. I have no alibi for Alison's murder. I

87

thought if I could get Lila to give me one I'd be off the hook. It's as simple as that."

"But that doesn't make sense! Why have her approach me? Why not the police?"

"She wasn't willing to lie to the police—make an official statement, perhaps go to court and swear on oath. But I thought if she could convince you I was innocent, it wouldn't be so bad. The cops might still suspect me, but as I didn't do it they could obviously never prove I did. And if you were batting for me . . . Well, you're a well-known person, a person of integrity. You've had experience with this sort of thing, you've cleared other people who were falsely accused. . . . If you were convinced of my innocence, then perhaps you'd nail the real killer."

He paused. "Besides, our friendship, your good opinion, means a lot to me. I couldn't bear to think of you believing me a killer."

"I never believed you were a killer," she insisted. "But I must admit that now I'm having doubts."

He looked at her in dismay. "Why? The evidence against me is no stronger now than it ever was."

"Innocent people don't normally bribe witnesses to prove their innocence."

"I didn't bribe her. I just persuaded her to do it as a favor to a friend."

"But what about the money in her purse?"

"I don't know a thing about it. Where would I get a thousand dollars?"

"Who said it was a thousand dollars?"

For perhaps five seconds he didn't answer. Then: "Andrews told me."

Jessica threw her hands up in despair. "Oh, David, I don't know. I want to believe you, I really do. But then there's that business of the phone call. Professor Lowery denies categorically having made it."

He said vehemently, "Jessica, I swear the call did come in. The caller said: 'This is Todd Lowery. Will you tell Mrs.'—"

Jessica cut in. "Hang on. You didn't say: 'Lowery's lying.' Your words were: 'The *caller* said.' "

"That's right."

"Does that mean you doubted it *was* Lowery?"

David frowned. "Not consciously at the time."

"But?"

"Well, thinking it over, the voice was odd. Of course, I don't really know Lowery. I've never been to his lectures; but I remember thinking the voice was strangely gruff. Naturally, I had no reason to believe there was anything wrong . . ."

"Strangely gruff: you mean as though it was disguised?"

He nodded. "Yes. It was—I don't know—unnaturally gruff."

Chapter Nine

THE next morning Jessica phoned Lieutenant Andrews. She detected a slight air of weariness in his voice as he answered. "Yes, Mrs. Fletcher, what can I do for you now?"

"I won't keep you a moment, Lieutenant, and I'm not interfering, but I may have some information on the Brevard case for you. However, first will you answer me one question: did you tell David Tolliver that Lila Schroeder had a thousand dollars in her purse when she died?"

"No, I didn't."

Jessica's heart sank. "That's what I feared," she said. "Then I do have something to tell you."

"Before you go on, Mrs. Fletcher, I should tell *you* the Brevard case is closed."

"I beg your pardon?" Jessica thought she had misheard.

"We've got our man."

Her heart missed a beat. "You've actually made an arrest?"

"Yep. And charged him."

"Well, who is it?" she asked excitedly.

He hesitated. Then he said: "Oh well, you may as well know. It'll be in the afternoon news in a couple of hours. His name's Eddie Griggs."

"Who?" Jessica exclaimed.

"He's a professional burglar, with a record of resorting to violence when cornered."

Jessica felt her theories about the case being turned upside down. "How did you get on to him? May I ask?"

"Burglary Division got a lead on some of the jewelry stolen from Alison Brevard's apartment. They backtracked from the fence to Griggs. When he was questioned, he suddenly broke down and made a full confession."

"Why should he do that?"

"Neurotic sort of guy. Never killed before. Riddled with guilt. He's confessed to a string of other burglaries, all from middle-aged rich women living alone—widows, divorcees. This job went wrong, and he just couldn't live with it."

"Forgive me, Lieutenant, but could there be any doubt? I mean, I know you often get false confessions, don't you?"

"Not in this case. There's no shadow of doubt. Griggs knew far too much about the incidental details of the case. Take my word for it."

"Oh, I do, Mr. Andrews."

"Of course, the Schroeder case is still wide open. Griggs didn't kill *her*. So if you have any info that ties in with that, please spill it."

Jessica didn't answer immediately. Her mind was working quickly. At last she said, "I don't."

"Are you sure, Mrs. Fletcher? Anything might be useful."

"I have nothing at the moment. I may later. I need to do some heavy thinking. I'll get back to you."

"Just keep it to thinking, will you? Don't go for any more nighttime prowls in empty warehouses. Or empty universities."

She said sharply, "You know about my accident?"

"I know about the attempt on your life, Mrs. Fletcher. And I'm warning you: take care."

Jessica spent the rest of that morning putting the finishing touches to her book. She typed the last few pages herself, packed up the manuscript, took it to the hotel post office, and mailed it. She felt then as if a great burden had been lifted from her. She also felt at a bit of a loose end, and didn't quite know what to do next.

She'd told Andrews she would do some serious thinking about the murder. But it was no use just sitting down, staring at the wall and hoping that enlightenment would strike. She needed to do something—something mechanical that would let her mind roam freely. Of course! She had shopping to do for the dinner she was going to cook at Edmund's that night.

She made her way to the nearest supermarket.

As she wandered along the aisles making her selection, it occurred to her that it might have been a bit pushy of her to suggest cooking a meal in Edmund's house. Perhaps he wouldn't want her there—in Gwen's kitchen. Too late to back out now.

Of course, on the other hand, he might well be looking forward to her visit. Surely he must get tired of constant restaurant meals. She reflected that his restaurant bills over the course of a year must be tremendous. Though very likely, if asked just how much, he wouldn't have a clue. She smiled. One would have to ask Amelia. It wasn't as though he patronized cheap restaurants, either. The one he'd taken her to the other night, though not as expensive as the one she'd gone to with David, must nevertheless have set him back a good few dollars. And the Lumberjack Inn, where he'd taken Lila, sounded like quite a swanky place, too. However, Edmund would probably regard those outings as special occasions.

Jessica reached out casually for a packet of flour. And as she did so she froze. She stood unmoving, aghast at the thought which had struck her.

Oh no . . . Impossible.

But even as she told herself this, she knew it was far from impossible. It was hideously possible.

Jessica's legs felt suddenly shaky. She continued to stand quite still. It took a woman's voice, whining irritably, "Pardon me," to bring her to her senses, and make her realize she was blocking the aisle with her shopping cart.

She moved away hastily, trying to pull herself together. She could hardly face the possibility that this idea might be true. But it all fitted—fitted with a beautiful kind of coherence and logic. And obviously she couldn't just forget it. Once a murder had been committed, others would probably follow. Indeed, an attempt at a second had almost certainly already been made. She was going to have to do something about it.

But what?

Jessica walked slowly but resolutely along the marbled corridor. There was a gnawing inside her, and her heart was beating like a steam hammer. It was not that she was frightened—she was pretty sure she faced no personal danger—but to accuse *anyone* of murder was a horrible thing, let alone someone who . . .

Jessica came up to a door and stopped. She drew a deep breath, then tapped on it. The name on the door was Dr. Edmund Gerard.

A voice called, "Come in."

Jessica entered. Amelia looked up from her desk with a smile. Without any preliminaries, Jessica asked abruptly, "Amelia, is the Dean in?"

"No, he's not."

Jessica didn't know whether to be glad or sorry. "Where is he, do you know?"

"Not exactly, right now. Is it important?"

"Yes," Jessica said. "Very important."

Amelia eyed her keenly. "Mrs. Fletcher, you don't look at all well."

"I don't *feel* well," Jessica said. She managed a weak smile. "Do you mind if I sit down?"

"Of course not." She got to her feet. "Can I get you some water?"

"No, I'll be all right if I can just sit here for a moment."

"What exactly is the trouble?" Amelia sat down again slowly.

Jessica looked at her. She hesitated. Then she gave her a helpless shrug. "It's no good. I have to tell somebody."

She moistened her lips. "Amelia, the police believe Edmund killed Lila Schroeder."

Amelia went white. "You—you can't be serious."

Jessica nodded dumbly.

"But why—I mean what . . . ?" She trailed off. "But he hardly knew her."

"Yes, he did," Jessica said. "He's been seeing her secretly for a couple of months."

Amelia gave a gasp. "I don't believe it!"

"I'm afraid it's true. He used to take her to that place outside of town—the Lumberjack Inn. You know?"

Amelia shook her head blankly.

"Oh, surely you must," Jessica insisted.

"I tell you I've never heard of it!" She spoke sharply.

"How odd." Jessica's tone was suddenly cold.

"What do you mean?"

"Well, you pay Edmund's credit card bills, don't you? It was what you were doing the first day I met you. And you check them all very carefully."

"So?" Amelia's voice had taken on a higher pitch.

"So I know for a fact that the first couple of times he went there he paid by credit card. You couldn't have missed those bills. Edmund told me no one knew he took Lila there. But you did."

"No—I—you're wrong," Amelia said vehemently.

"You're the only one who *could* have known, Amelia," Jessica said quietly. "When you came across those bills, you could probably tell from their totals that they covered dinner for two. And you must have realized Edmund was seeing another woman surreptitiously; after all, if the thing was aboveboard, why should he take his guest all that way out of town, at least two times? I think you became obsessed with discovering who this woman was. So much so that you started following Edmund around to try to find out. One night you followed when he took the girl out to the Lumberjack again. And you followed them back to Seattle afterward. Perhaps you still hadn't got close enough to identify her; so when Edmund and she separated, you followed her cab. Then when she got out and started crossing the road, you tried to run her down." She paused. "I'm right, aren't I?"

Amelia said nothing. She seemed dazed, bemused, almost hypnotized by Jessica's low-level voice and steady gaze.

Jessica waited for several seconds, then continued remorselessly. "You missed on that occasion. But you had at last seen her face and knew who she was. You were horrified. That Edmund should take up with an empty-headed little tramp like Lila Schroeder . . . and you were eaten up with jealousy. You started following Lila around instead of Edmund. You knew you had to get rid of her, not only for your own sake, but for Edmund's: you couldn't let her mess up his life as she had other men's. It was almost a duty to save him. You only had to wait for the right opportunity. And it came the other night when she drove out to the docks. Alone. You probably thought she was going to meet Edmund. You followed her into the warehouse. When she heard you coming, she no doubt thought you were me. She came toward you—and you struck at her with that longshoreman's hook. Then you heard my taxi approaching, ran to your own car and got away just before I arrived."

Again she stopped. Amelia was still staring speechlessly at her. Her eyes were wild; guilt was written all over her face. Jessica realized the tremendous pressure the woman was under, the almost irresistible urge to talk—to tell someone about her crimes. Yet, still she resisted. Jessica knew that if she came through this crisis, her resolve would be strengthened and she would probably never confess. And, with the evidence against her as flimsy as it was, she might never even come to trial.

Jessica called on all the persuasiveness of her command. She spoke softly but compellingly. "Amelia, you did all this for Edmund. Don't let him suffer now because of it. Tell the truth. Think how much better you'll feel after. No more lies. No more concealment. . . ."

For long seconds she waited. The muscles of Amelia's face were twitching. And then suddenly it all came bursting out.

"I didn't plan it," she gasped. "I didn't go there meaning to kill her. I thought she'd gone to meet Edmund again. I had to know. I followed her into the warehouse and she spotted me. She guessed why I was there. She started to laugh—jeer at me. She called me a frustrated old maid. She said she was going to tell Edmund. I couldn't take it. I snatched up that hook thing and lashed out at her. She . . . she stopped laughing."

She stared pleadingly at Jessica. "If I'd planned to kill her, I'd have taken a weapon with me, wouldn't I? I wouldn't have relied on finding something just lying around."

Jessica didn't answer. She felt physically and mentally drained. She raised her voice.

"You can come in now, Lieutenant."

The door, which she'd left an inch ajar behind her, swung wide open and Andrews and his sergeant stood there.

Amelia looked at them. She didn't seem at all surprised to see them. "I suppose you want me to come with you?" she asked quietly.

"If you please, ma'am. Read her her rights, Lou."

The sergeant took a card from his pocket and read out the familiar words. When he'd finished, Amelia whispered, "I understand. My coat, please."

She pointed to the back of the door. Andrews turned away to get it, and as he did so Edmund pushed his way into the room and between the two policemen. His face was flushed. He stared at Amelia.

"You heard?" asked Amelia.

He nodded. "They made me wait outside. Amelia—*why*?"

"Because I loved you."

He shook his head helplessly. "I had no idea."

"No." Her voice was bitter. "None at all. Even after all these years. Even after Gwen died. I was an adjunct to your life—only a little more useful than a piece of office furniture."

"That's not true. I valued your friendship deeply."

"So you took up with that girl."

"Amelia, Lila meant nothing to me. It was a passing thing. I could have handled it."

Andrews held out Amelia's coat and she slipped into it. She stared coolly at Edmund.

"Are you sure?" she said. Then she added: "And what about her?" She nodded at Jessica.

"There's nothing like that between Jessica and me," he said.

"So she told me. And for a while I believed her. Then I heard you talking outside that door the other day: saying you wanted a serious talk with her; arranging for her to come and cook dinner at your house. I asked you to have dinner at my place twice after Gwen died. Or, I said, I'd come to you. You turned me down."

"So for that reason you lured her to the English building by pretending to be Todd Lowery and pushed her down the stairs?" He was incredulous.

Amelia didn't answer. After a moment Andrews touched her on the shoulder. "Let's go."

The sergeant led the way out of the room. Without a backward glance, Amelia followed. Andrews went last, closing the door behind him. Three seconds later he opened it again.

"Mrs. Fletcher?"

She glanced up wearily. "Yes?"

"Thanks."

He closed the door a second time. Edmund and Jessica remained in silence—he standing, she sitting—for about half a minute. Then he stepped across to her.

"Jess, you look dead beat."

She raised her face. There were tears in her eyes. She spoke with intensity.

"Edmund, I hate this, I hate it!"

"It is pretty horrible."

"People mustn't be allowed to get away with it," she said. "Because they're unhappy or frightened or worried or jealous or can't control their tempers, they mustn't be allowed to get away with murder. I know that. Yet every time, the temptation to let them—just to keep quiet—is tremendous. I feel so cruel.''

He smiled. ''You, cruel? You're joking, of course.''

''I don't feel like joking.'' Then she took a deep breath. ''Anyway, let's not talk about it anymore. At least for now.''

She got to her feet. ''Edmund, will you come to the supermarket with me? If I'm going to cook you that meal tonight, there are things to buy. I started earlier, but I had to break off.''

He frowned. ''Supermarket? Is that one of those places where you help yourself to goods from the shelves?'' Then, as she stared at him, he smiled again. ''Jessica, I live in an academic ivory tower, remember? I wouldn't know about such things.''

Chapter Ten

JESSICA sat reading in the airport departure lounge, waiting for her flight to Kentucky to be called. Edmund, who had a full day's engagements, had been unable to come and see her off. She was not sorry, because she preferred not to be waved off at railroad stations and airports. They had said their goodbyes the previous evening, after she had at last prepared for him his home-cooked dinner.

"Jessica, I've caught you," a voice said breathlessly.

Startled, she looked up. Standing smiling down at her was David.

"I phoned the hotel and they told me what plane you were catching. I thought I wouldn't make it."

She looked up at the clock. "I have just ten minutes."

"Fancy leaving without giving me a chance to say a proper thank-you."

"For what?"

"Without you I might have been convicted of murder."

"Oh, I doubt that."

He sat down next to her. "Jessica, we haven't much time, so can we cut out the polite repartee? You know how I feel about you."

"No, I don't; and I'm not sure I want to."

"Well, the truth is that you're a fascinating woman and I'm enormously attracted to you."

"The way you were attracted to Alison Brevard?" she asked.

99

He looked hurt. "Oh, that's not fair! I've explained how things were between Alison and me."

"And the others?"

"What others?" His expression was blank.

"David, stop pretending."

He shrugged. "All right, there've been a couple of others. Look, I can't help it, but I find myself attracted to mature women, particularly if they're bright and funny—"

"And rich?"

He flushed. "That has nothing to do with it. The most important thing is intelligent conversation. And I like a woman I can learn from. I mean, take the way you've opened my eyes about crime fiction: it's a whole new interest for me now."

He put his hand on hers. "Jessica, I've read all your books in a week. I'm crazy about them. I'd just love to be involved with your work."

"As my typist?"

He spread his hands. "Sure! You know I'm good. But I'd hope not to be exclusively a typist, for always. Jessica, I'm sure there are dozens of ways I could be useful to you."

She regarded him appraisingly. "Well," she said, "I'll tell you what I do lack: somebody I can try my ideas out on before I even start writing. There's nobody in Cabot Cove whose literary judgment I can really rely on."

He grinned. "Well, I'd be perfect for that. I'm a good judge of literature."

"Very well," she said slowly, "let's have a test. Let me try out a scenario on you. Tell me what you think of it."

"New?"

"Yes."

"Great. But is there time?"

"Oh, it'll only take a few minutes. Right, let me see. The principal character of this story is a young man. Very good-looking. Talented. Charming. And highly attractive to women."

"Lucky guy."

"Older women especially find him almost irresistible. He soon learns how to use this . . . this gift. There are many lonely, wealthy older women around; and being of an unscrupulous nature, he exploits this situation for all it's worth. Such women are usually generous, and the young man starts doing pretty well for himself. But not quite well enough. For our protagonist is greedy.

"Now, he is a student journalist and spends a lot of time at the courthouse, reporting cases, interviewing prisoners. In this way he meets a man who is shortly to be paroled after serving a term for burglary. And he gets a brilliant idea. He cultivates the acquaintance of this man—let's call him Teddy Briggs—and finds out all he can about him. He learns that Briggs is insecure, slightly neurotic, has a tendency to panic in an emergency and to use violence. But his technique as a burglar is first-class. And he's extremely loyal to his associates. It's a perfect setup, and eventually the two go into partnership. Our charming young man cases the homes of his wealthy lady friends—finds out what valuables they keep there, their safe combinations, details of security devices installed. Perhaps our protagonist is even able to make impressions of their front door keys. Then, on a particular evening he takes the lady for a long night out—out of town. When she returns in the early hours she finds her home stripped.

"This extremely lucrative racket continues for some months. The ladies don't suspect our young charmer of involvement—or, if they do, they keep quiet about it. Most of them are rather embarrassed about their friendship with a younger man and so don't tell the police whom they were out with on the night of the crime. Also, they don't talk about the relationship to their friends—and he's thus able to string several women along at the same time.

"However, after a while things start to go wrong. He takes up with a woman—we'll call her Alice—who isn't embarrassed by the relationship. She talks about it. She even pins his photo up in her apartment. Moreover, she's clinging: she demands more and more of his time. Worst of all, she's an alcoholic. She becomes a real pest—and a potential threat. Because she makes it clear that, in spite of her infatuation with him, she doesn't really trust the young man. He knows he can't afford to take any risks where she's concerned. At the same time Briggs is harassing him—keeps demanding the information he needs to burglarize Alice's apartment. The young man begins to get desperate. He wants to be rid of both Briggs and Alice. But how?

"Then he has an idea. Briggs has used violence in the past. The young man could never use violence himself. But he has no objection to others using it. He couldn't actually organize it or order it. But with this scheme he doesn't have to. All he has to do is give Briggs the information he needs about Alice's apartment, arrange a date with Alice one evening, notify Briggs—but then not turn up for the date.

"Of course, it's a hit-and-miss plan. He doesn't know what will happen. Perhaps nothing. But it's likely Alice will go home early and catch Briggs in the act. Then . . . who knows? She might call the police and Briggs might be arrested. Or Briggs might kill her. It's just possible Briggs will kill her *and* be arrested. So there's a fair chance our young man will get either Alice or Briggs off his back— perhaps even both of them. Anyway, he's a gambler. It's worth a try. And the beauty of it is that he doesn't have to do anything, just stay at home studying and leave the outcome to fate.

"Well, his plan works—to an extent. Briggs does kill Alice. But he gets away. However, his nerve is broken and he has to lie low for a bit. No more jobs. Our young man thinks his troubles are over. The one possibility, though, which in his conceit had not occurred to him, was that he himself would be suspected of Alice's murder . . ."

Throughout this recital David had remained perfectly silent and still. His eyes were fixed on Jessica's face. The only signs of emotion were some beads of sweat on his upper lip. And his body was tense.

"Well, what do you think?" she asked.

He made a clearly conscious effort to relax. He smiled. But it was a travesty of his old smile.

"Fascinating," he said. "Though a little farfetched, don't you think?"

Jessica shrugged. "Perhaps. Of course, it's all merely a product of my imagination." She cocked her head. "Ah, that's my flight being called."

She picked up her purse from the seat and her attaché case from the floor and got to her feet.

"Well, goodbye, David." She started to turn away.

"Jessica!"

She stopped. "Yes?"

"What happens to the young man?"

"I don't know, David. You decide."

And Jessica walked briskly away in the direction of the departure gate.

Chapter Eleven

ABBY Freestone's compact foreign car drew to a halt outside the big iron gate. Jessica, in the passenger seat, expected her cousin to get out, or at least sound the horn, but for about five seconds Abby just remained behind the wheel. Then the gate slowly opened. It did not swing wide, but slid back like an elevator door, with a rumbling of rollers on metal tracks. Abby drove through the gateway, raising a hand in acknowledgment as she did so.

Jessica looked sideways at her in bewilderment. "Who did you wave to?"

"Barnes, the security guard. Or his assistant."

"I didn't see him."

Abby laughed and stopped the car. "Look back—out the window."

Jessica did as instructed, craning her head around. "I still don't see anyone."

"Have a look up that tree to the right of the gate."

Jessica squinted upward. Through the foliage her eyes spotted something black and angular. "Is that a camera?" she asked.

"That's right. Closed-circuit TV. Sometimes one has to use the intercom to call up the security room; but if Barnes is watching his monitor, it's usually not necessary."

Jessica drew her head back into the car. "Well, goodness me."

"Surely you've seen security cameras before?" Abby got the car moving again.

"Yes, of course—in department stores, banks, offices, even apartment buildings in big cities. Here it seems wrong somehow. Out of place."

She gestured around. The wide graveled drive was curving between large close-cropped paddocks enclosed by immaculate white fencing. Elegant, glossy-coated horses grazed or frisked. The sun shone brilliantly. Birds sang. Somewhere in the distance a dog was barking. It was all very rural and peaceful.

Abby gave a nod. "I know what you mean. But believe me, it's very necessary here."

Before Jessica could ask her what she meant, the car rounded a clump of trees and Abby announced: "Langley Manor. What do you think of it?"

The house gleamed a vivid white in the afternoon sun. It was colonnaded and seemed to have spread itself luxuriously over the ground with a confidence born in an earlier age's sense of limitless space and limitless money.

"It's lovely," Jessica said softly.

Abby drove around the back of the house and through a stable yard lined by stalls; over the closed lower half-doors, the heads of several more horses eyed them curiously.

Abby drew up in front of a snug-looking, picturesque little cottage beyond the stable yard and they both got out. Abby marched to the rear of the car, opened the trunk and heaved out the larger of Jessica's suitcases.

"Oh, Abby," Jessica said hastily, "that's too heavy!" But her cousin ignored her.

"Bosh," she said cheerfully. "I'm the hearty, outdoor member of the family, remember? You're the indoor, bookish type. You take the little one."

"I'm nothing of the sort," Jessica told her indignantly. "I'll have you know I jog every day at home—and cycle everywhere."

But Abby had disappeared into the house. Jessica picked up the smaller case and followed.

A moment later she was looking with pleasure around the low-ceilinged living room of the cottage. There was a big open fireplace, cretonne covers on the easy chairs, chintz drapes at the windows, horse brasses on the walls. The table and the dining chairs were of dark polished mahogany.

"It looks very English, Abby," she said.

"Well, I've tried to make it a home away from home. However olde-worlde it may be, it's got all modern conveniences, even indoor plumbing. Come on, I'll show you your room, then you can freshen up while I make some tea."

Fifteen minutes later Jessica was seated deep in one of the comfortable old easy chairs, gratefully sipping a cup of steaming Earl Grey and nibbling at a cake. Abby poured herself a cup, sat down opposite, kicked off her shoes and tucked her legs up under her. She drank some tea and gave a sigh. "Ah, I needed that!"

Jessica regarded her with an expression of slightly amused affection. In spite of her forty years and athletic build, there was still something very schoolgirlish about Abigail Freestone. Her round, rosy-cheeked, well-scrubbed face, apparently completely devoid of makeup, glowed with health. Her shiny light brown hair was tied back in a loose bun. She was wearing a shirt, a sleeveless pullover and corduroy trousers. She looked utterly relaxed and contented.

"Abby," Jessica said, "I feel very guilty. Ever since you met me at the airport, I seem to have been talking about myself—my books, my adventures. I've hardly asked a thing about you."

"But your life is so much more exciting than mine, Jess. I was dying to hear about everything."

"Well, I want to hear about you now. I must say you look very well and happy."

"Oh, I am. This job's a dream come true. Denton gives me a completely free hand with the horses. And the facilities are super."

"How did you happen to land the job?"

"I met Denton years ago when he came to England as an official with the American show-jumping team. Then about a year ago I had this letter, out of the blue, asking me to take over the training of his horses. I was staggered. Of course I jumped at it. Oh, Jess, he's a marvelous man. He doesn't treat me like an employee at all: just like—'' She broke off.

"One of the family?" Jessica finished.

"No, not really. Better."

Jessica raised her eyebrows. "Really? Doesn't he treat his family well?"

"My dear, it's not his fault. They're awful, they really are. They've got no interest in the stables or the estate. If you ask me, they're just waiting for him to die so they can sell everything and carve up the loot."

Abby's eyes flashed. Her expression was suddenly angry. Jessica surveyed her thoughtfully. Then Abby looked a little abashed.

"Perhaps I'm being a bit hard. I don't suppose they actually *want* him to die. But they can't wait to get their hands on the dough."

"Who do *they* consist of?" Jessica asked.

"Well, there's Spenser. He's the son. About my age, or a bit younger. He's one of these sharp operators—only interested in the fast buck. Always seems to be involved in some scheme I can't understand, but which definitely sounds shady. At the moment he's in some sort of PR work, I think—lobbying on behalf of one of those Arab organizations. Denton says they're nothing but terrorists. Spenser's got a lot of charm when he wants it, but it's all quite spurious. I think he's just a glorified con man. He really ought to have been a Mississippi riverboat cardsharp about a hundred years ago."

Jessica smiled. "Right, that's Spenser very succinctly summed up. Who else is there?"

"Two daughters. Morgana and Trish."

Jessica frowned. "Trish Langley. That seems to ring a bell."

Abby nodded meaningfully. "The Hollingsworth case. Trish was the other woman."

"Oh, of course." Jessica remembered the acrimonious and highly publicized divorce of the multimillionaire Jeremy Hollingsworth and his high-society wife several years earlier.

"Hollingsworth dropped her like a hotcake afterwards," Abby went on, "and according to her, she didn't get a penny out of him. She still looks on herself as one of the smart set, though: it's casinos and nightclubs half the year, running through her allowance; and then home the other half, sucking up to Daddy and hoping to cadge another few thousand dollars to keep her in strong liquor and weak men. She throws herself into everything when she's home— even comes hunting. But you should see the expression of utter boredom on her face sometimes!"

Abby helped herself to a cake from a plate on a low table between them and bit into it hungrily.

"And the other daughter . . . Morgana, did you say?"

Abby nodded, swallowed a lump of cake, and swigged some tea. Then she said, "Mrs. Morgana Langley-Cramer. She's divorced. Morgana's harmless enough, but quite loopy."

"Oh, in what way?"

"She's into all that supernatural stuff: spiritualism, fortune-telling, astrology—you know."

"Yes, I know," Jessica said, "I've met people like that."

"She just floats around in a sort of daze, mumbling about astral projection and the great pyramid—all that sort of thing. Though I sometimes get the impression she may be just a little more astute than she seems on the surface. Not that Echo seems to think so; she treats Morgana with a kind of pitying condescension."

Jessica's eyes widened. "Who or what is Echo?"

"Morgana's daughter."

"You did say *Echo?*"

"Yes; priceless, isn't it?"

"Does she keep coming back?"

Abby gave a chortle. "She does, actually. But only because her mother insists: she's the only grandchild and Morgana won't let her risk getting cut out of the will. She's a punk."

Jessica laughed. "Really?"

"Yes, though at the moment she's going through a conservative phase: she's got her hair cut very short and dyed snow-white, not green or mauve this time. And she hasn't got a safety pin through her nose, or anything."

"That must be a relief to everyone."

"Actually, I rather like Echo," Abby said. "She's honest; doesn't attempt to disguise her boredom or her contempt for her Aunt Trish and Uncle Spenser. And, believe it or not, she has a very good seat on a horse. In the blood, I suppose. I think she could be a fine rider—if she could just forget that horses typify all the conventional upper-class values she despises."

"You're becoming quite a psychologist, Abby."

Abby looked rather embarrassed. "Gosh, no. I understand horses and dogs better than people, really. You'll probably tell me I'm quite wrong about them all when you meet them."

"They're all here now, are they?"

"Yes, they're not often all present at the same time, but it's a special occasion on Thursday. Denton's birthday. There's going to be a meet here to celebrate it."

"A meet of the hunt?"

"Yes, there'll be the traditional hunt breakfast first, complete with a punch bowl."

"Should be fun," Jessica said. "Perhaps they'll be able to use the television cameras to locate the fox."

"Oh, Jess, you must say that to Denton. He'll love it."

"I've been meaning to ask you: what did you mean when you said all this security was very necessary here?"

"The paintings, of course."

"Oh, does Denton have a collection?"

"My dear, they're valued at over three million dollars."

"Indeed?" Jessica looked impressed.

"Are you surprised? I thought you realized he's very well off."

"Oh, I did. I just didn't associate him with art treasures."

"Now, don't get it wrong, Jess. There's none of this modern abstract nonsense. The pictures are good old-fashioned country scenes: animals, birds, horses. But first-class. All the experts say so.''

"I see: Landseer, Munnings, people like that?''

"Very probably.''

Jessica concealed a smile.

"Anyway,'' Abby continued, "you'll see them all tonight and be able to judge for yourself.''

"*Tonight*?'' Jessica stared.

"Yes. Denton's invited us both over to dinner. Didn't I tell you?''

"No, you did not.'' Jessica spoke a trifle grimly.

"Sorry.'' Abby sounded quite unapologetic. "Of course, I've been boasting so much about my cousin, the famous author, and he's longing to meet you. So's Tom and—''

Jessica interrupted. "Whoa! Tom?''

"Tom Cassidy. Oh, you'll love him. He's Denton's oldest friend. Farms six hundred acres next door. Then again, Mr. Boswell says he's got some ideas for you—real-life cases he's come across that he says would make super mystery stories.''

Jessica raised a hand. She spoke ominously. "And who is Mr. Boswell?''

"Oh, Marcus Boswell—Denton's lawyer.''

Jessica closed her eyes. "Abby,'' she asked quietly, "are all these people coming to meet me?''

"I don't know what you mean by *all*: only Tom and Mr. Boswell are coming specially. The others would be there anyway.''

"I'm guest of honor, aren't I?'' Jessica's tone was exasperated.

"It's not going to be anything as formal as that,'' Abby said defensively.

"But that's what it amounts to?''

Abby wriggled awkwardly. "Well . . . sort of—''

"Oh, really, Abby! I came here to get away from all that sort of thing.''

"I say, do you mind awfully? I'm sorry, Jess. Denton has his heart set on it. There are only going to be nine of us. And it's given me a lot of clout with Spense and Trish, having a famous cousin. Until now they've looked on me as just a country bumpkin.''

Jessica relented. She laughed. ''No, I don't really mind, Abby. I suppose it's flattering. It's just that I could have done with a day or two to rest up and settle in before going on display.''

''All right, then, I'll ask Denton to put it off for a bit.''

''No, no, I wouldn't hear of it. If I could just lie down for an hour or so first? I always find air travel so exhausting, and I don't think I've completely recovered from that fall I told you about.''

''Yes, you do that. I've got to go and look at a couple of the horses anyway.'' She got to her feet. ''We'll get a jolly good blowout up at the big house, anyway. Much better than I could knock up in my little kitchen. So count your blessings, old girl.''

Chapter Twelve

"**WELL**, there you are, Mrs. Fletcher, that's about the lot. What do you think?"

Denton Langley spoke with just the faintest tone of pride.

"I'm very impressed indeed, Mr. Langley," Jessica said.

And it was true. The paintings covered nearly every spare foot of wall space in the hallway and main staircase of Langley Manor. They included two Landseers, a small, early Constable and a Whistler, as well as a host of works by somewhat lesser artists, which were nonetheless of first-rate quality.

"Well, I don't claim to be an expert on art," Langley said, "but I do know these fellows' *subjects*. And the one thing they have in common is that they've gotten their subjects just right. That's my criterion. And the art experts seem to agree with me."

"I'm sure one could spend hours studying them with great pleasure."

"Well, feel free to stop by anytime and browse as long as you're here."

"Why, thank you, Mr. Langley."

"And call me Denton, please. Nothing makes a man of my age forget his years like hearing a young woman call him by his first name."

"And nothing makes a woman of my age forget her years like hearing a man call her young."

"You're young to me, my dear. I bet I could give you twenty-five years."

"Oh, I'm sure that's not true."

"How old do you think I am?"

"Well, really, I couldn't say." Jessica was a little flustered.

"Eighty this week."

She gazed at the tall, soldierly figure. Denton Langley's hair was white, but his face was unlined and his eyes bright. His back was ramrod straight, and he moved with a speed and suppleness that would have done credit to a man of sixty.

"I find that hard to believe," she said truthfully.

He looked pleased. "You must spend as much time as you can here, Mrs. Fletcher."

"Jessica."

"Well, Jessica, if you've seen enough of these for now, let's go and have a drink."

He gave her his arm and escorted her across the great square hallway and into the beautifully proportioned and elegantly finished living room. Here Abby was standing, clutching a glass and chatting somewhat uneasily with a man whom Jessica had already met briefly before Denton had swept her off on a tour of his art collection. This was her host's son, Spenser.

As she approached him now, Jessica appreciated afresh the aptness of Abby's likening him to a Mississippi card-sharp. Spenser Langley was as tall as his father, but less erect and somehow softer looking. His face was pale, high cheek-boned, and his light blue eyes had a transparent quality. He wore a strangely old-fashioned narrow mustache. His movements were slow and graceful. His smile came quick and often.

"Ah, tour over, Mrs. Fletcher?" he asked.

"For the moment."

"What can I get you to drink?"

"Could I have a dry sherry?"

"Coming up."

He glided over to a drinks cabinet against one wall. Abby looked slightly relieved, and relaxed a little.

Denton addressed Jessica. "I must admit I'm not much of a literary man, but Abby loaned me a couple of yours, and I enjoyed 'em no end."

"Thank you, sir."

"Tell me one thing." Jessica braced herself. "How on earth do you think up—?"

But fortunately, at that moment there was an interruption. Three women entered the room through the big double doors at the far end.

Denton turned toward them. "Ah, girls, come and meet our guest of honor."

The three advanced across the expanse of carpet. The first was about thirty. She was petite, slim and very attractive, with long blonde hair that gave no indication of being dyed. She had the same high cheekbones as Spenser. But her movements were quick and jerky, and her eyes, also blue, were constantly on the move, seeming never to alight on anything for more than a second.

"My daughter Trish," Denton said.

Trish's face lit up—just too much. "Darling," she drawled, "it's wonderful to meet you at last! I just adore your gorgeous little books."

She held out a rather clawlike hand with bloodred nails. Jessica took it somewhat gingerly. But she'd hardly touched it before Trish was turning and saying to her brother, who had just approached: "Spense, give me a big, big martini. At least a treble."

Spenser handed Jessica a glass of sherry, glancing sardonically at his sister as he did so. "Thought you said *big*, Trish. Surely you don't consider a mere treble big?"

She made a face at him. "Oh, funny, funny. Just start pouring and shut up."

Meanwhile Denton was saying, "And this is my elder daughter, Morgana."

A shorter woman pushed herself close up to Jessica and peered at her out of narrowed eyes. She had a pleasant, good-natured, rather stupid face. Her makeup was carelessly applied, and her hair a mass of untidy curls. Cheap-looking, chunky jewelry dripped from her: heavy drop earrings in the form of signs of the zodiac, a big scarab brooch, several charm bracelets and about eight rings—also bearing zodiac emblems. She gripped Jessica's hand tightly, pressing the rings painfully into her flesh. She gave a beatific smile, her gaze shifting to a spot about six inches above Jessica's right shoulder. "You have a very strong aura, my dear," she said.

Jessica smiled weakly. "Oh, have I? That's good."

Morgana cocked her head, as though listening, before continuing. "Running Elk says you are a true medium."

Jessica thought rapidly. "Your spirit guide?" she hazarded.

Morgana looked pleased. "Precisely. He's right behind you. You can hear him?"

Resisting a strong impulse to glance over her shoulder, Jessica said, "I'm afraid not."

"You will. Give it time. Don't worry."

"I'm not worrying." Jessica told her.

Morgana peered again into Jessica's face. "Gemini?" she asked abruptly.

"Er, actually, no. I'm—"

Morgana cut in. "Don't tell me. Let me think." She closed her eyes.

For the last few seconds, Denton had been making impatient harrumphing noises under his breath; he sounded rather like an anxious horse. Now he said hastily, "And this is my granddaughter, Echo."

He almost brushed Morgana to one side and tried to usher forward the girl who'd been standing in the background. But Echo didn't budge. She just glowered.

"How do you do?" Jessica said brightly.

"Hi." Still Echo didn't smile. With her short, spiky white hair, she had affected an almost equally white pancake makeup, and big scarlet lips. But at least she had no abstract designs painted on her cheeks, and her dress was quite plain, almost drab.

Jessica held out her hand, virtually forcing the girl to

step forward and take it. Echo cast a glance at her mother, who had moved away to join Spenser and Trish. She then said defiantly, "Mother's not insane."

"Echo!" Denton spoke sharply.

"I never assumed she was," Jessica assured her.

"Oh, but all that about Running Elk—you must have thought—"

"If your mother can see a Red Indian standing behind me, who am I to say there's no one there?"

A glimmer of a smile started on Echo's face, but just then there came another interruption as the butler from the doorway announced: "Mr. Cassidy!"

A big, lumbering, jovial-looking man in his sixties bustled across the room. He had a red face and thinning sandy hair.

"Ah, Tom," said Denton in a relieved voice.

Tom Cassidy grinned. "Hi, Dent."

"Tom, meet the famous Jessica Fletcher."

Tom stuck out a huge brown hand and enveloped Jessica's in it. "So you're little Abby's cousin," he said. "We've sure heard a lot about you."

He was as tall as the Langley men, but broader in the shoulders, and altogether beefier. He still had a look of sheer physical strength about him. Jessica found herself wondering if all the men in this part of the world were tall.

The question was answered a few minutes later when Marcus Boswell, the lawyer, was shown into the room. He was a short, stocky, dapper man with small regular features, slicked-down black hair, and the air of somehow being busy even when making small talk over a cocktail.

It was after they'd all been doing this for a further fifteen minutes that the butler announced dinner and they trooped into the dining room.

The meal, as Abby had forecast, was sustantial and good. Jessica noticed that, for one so spiritually-minded, Morgana had a surprisingly healthy appetite; that Echo merely played with her food; and that Trish ate little more than her niece, but compensated for this by drinking at least eight glasses of wine during the meal. She also observed that Spenser seemed definitely nervous and looked to be worried about something.

After dinner they returned to the living room. They were chatting quietly over their coffee when they were interrupted by the sound from the hall of an eager and impatient barking.

"Oh, there's that damn dog!" Denton exclaimed. "Sorry. Robert'll shut him up in a moment. He's got to learn he can't come in when I have guests—especially eminent lady novelists."

"Oh, please don't keep him out on my account," Jessica said hastily.

Denton looked gratified. "You sure?"

"Quite sure. I like dogs."

"Oh, very well. Echo, my dear, will you let him in?"

Echo went toward the door. "Really, Father," Trish said testily, "he'll be jumping up all over everyone."

"Not now, he won't. Abby's been working on him."

Echo opened the door and the dog came in excitedly. He was a young bright-eyed beagle, about six months old. He went frisking across to Denton, whose eyes softened as he bent down to fondle the dog's head.

"Hello, Teddy, old boy, how are you?" he murmured.

Teddy gave a little yelp and wagged his tail hard.

"Come on, boy, meet a new friend," Denton said. He led the dog to Jessica's chair and said, "Sit."

Teddy sat in front of her. "Shake, boy," Denton ordered, and the dog raised his right front paw.

Jessica put out her hand and shook it solemnly. "How do you do, Teddy? I'm pleased to meet you."

Teddy gave another little *wuff*. Next he suddenly spun on his tail, ran to Marcus Boswell, briefly thrust a nose into his hand, scampered from him to Abby, looked at her, then sat up and begged.

Denton chuckled. "He wants a reward from his trainer. Here." He took a sugar lump from the bowl on the table and handed it to her. She fed it to the dog, who crunched it up with relish.

"I never thought he'd remember me," Marcus Boswell said. He sounded quite touched.

"Teddy was a present from Marcus after my old dog died last year," Denton explained to Jessica. He patted the dog's head.

"You've done wonders with him, Abby," Tom Cassidy told her.

She shrugged. "All by kindness. Actually, he's a remarkably intelligent dog and very easy to train."

Teddy obviously knew he was being talked about and thoroughly enjoyed being the center of attention. He gazed around the circle proudly, his tail thumping the floor. Jessica could have sworn he was smiling. However, when the conversation became general again, he lay down with a disgusted air and went to sleep.

Tom Cassidy said, "Understand you'll be coming out with us Thursday, Mrs. Fletcher."

"Oh, I don't really think so," Jessica said diffidently.

Denton looked disappointed. "Come, come, Jessica; Abby told us you'd be sure to want to join in. Mustn't be modest, you know."

Jessica cast her cousin a withering look. "It's just that I haven't been in the saddle for so many years . . ."

"Oh, that's nothing. We'll soon get you back into the swing. Abby can put you up on one of the old mares tomorrow and take you hacking gently around the estate. In a day you'll be rarin' to go, and on Thursday you'll be leading the field over the fences."

"I'm afraid there's no chance of that, at all. If I trot sedately around at the back of the field, that'll be the extent of it."

He chuckled. "We'll see, we'll see." He glanced her up and down appreciatively. "I know a natural horse-woman when I see one."

"Let's hope the horse does, too," Jessica replied.

Jessica spent the next day quietly. She slept late, read for a while, and then watched her cousin schooling some of the horses. Abby introduced her to an elderly, placid mare called Doughnut (named from her having, as a foal, devoured a bag of them left carelessly lying around by a stable boy; it was a name that somehow suited her).

Jessica also made the acquaintance of the hitherto invisible Barnes, who proudly showed her his security room, with its bank of television screens, intercom system and row of buttons operating the various gates leading on to the estate. Later she met his assistant, a somewhat taciturn individual named Smedley.

Later in the afternoon Abby persuaded Jessica to don a riding habit (a number of spare outfits were kept around the place for visitors) and mount Doughnut. They then went for a quiet amble on horseback around the estate. It felt strange, after so many years, to be on a horse again, but she soon found herself regaining the feel of it.

At one stage they came upon Echo. She was sitting on the grass under a tree, smoking a cigarette. When she spotted them, she hastily thrust the cigarette down into the soil at the foot of the tree. Jessica frowned. That cigarette hadn't looked entirely normal. As a former high school teacher she was unfortunately all too proficient at recognizing marijuana. She wondered if it was her duty to tell someone. But whom? It would surely be pointless to inform Morgana. Besides, the girl wasn't a child. And Jessica was sick of interfering in other people's lives. She would *not* let herself become a busybody.

Abby broke in on her thoughts. "Come on, let's try a canter."

"Oh no," Jessica said quickly. "Really, I don't think I'm quite—"

But Abby just reached over and gave Doughnut a slap on the flank. The mare broke into a canter and suddenly Jessica found herself clinging on for dear life.

Chapter Thirteen

BY that evening, Jessica, though stiff and sore, was feeling much more confident on horseback; and was beginning to think that—provided she didn't try anything too spectacular in the jumping line—she might get through Thursday morning unscathed.

When the day actually came, much of this confidence seemed, however, to have deserted her. She was feeling quite nervous when, smartly attired in her riding habit, she walked over to the manor house for the traditional hunt breakfast. She was on her own, as Abby had been up and working since five-thirty.

Outside the house swarmed a hive of activity. People on horseback, on foot, even on bicycles, milled excitedly among the dozens of parked cars—mostly Cadillacs, Mercedes and Jaguars—which were parked everywhere. More were arriving all the time. Jessica went indoors.

The breakfast was being held in the fine, spacious ballroom, which was already crowded with guests. The tables were loaded with food and drink, including a huge punch bowl, and the complexions on some of the faces present indicated that quite a few stirrup cups had already been quaffed.

Jessica slipped in unobtrusively, looking about hopefully for a coffeepot. The first familiar face she spotted was that of Trish, who was standing very close to a thin, nervous-looking young man. She was clinging to his arm and smiling up at him. As Jessica watched, she whispered into his ear. He flushed, and she gave a raucous laugh that turned several heads in her direction.

A moment later the tall, elegant figure of Spenser elbowed his way unceremoniously through the crowd and addressed the young man. "Anthony, we're awfully sorry your wife couldn't make it today." Then, looking pointedly at his sister, he added: "Aren't we, Trish?"

Trish's eyes flashed. Then quietly, but in extremely impolite terms, she invited her brother to depart. Jessica could not hear the words, but the movement of the girl's lips clearly indicated the phrase used. An expression of disgust appeared on Spenser's face and he turned abruptly away.

Just then Jessica became aware that Echo had drifted up to her. "Hi," the girl said shortly.

Jessica was pleasantly surprised. Echo had until now shown not the slightest sign of wishing to be friendly. So she smiled more broadly than usual in response. "Good morning, my dear."

She was just reflecting that, with the punkish hairdo topping the strictly conservative riding gear, Denton's granddaughter certainly stood out from the crowd, when Echo jerked her head over her shoulder. "The pits, aren't they?" she said.

Jessica was startled. "Er, who—what—?" she began incoherently.

"Spense and Trish. My revered uncle and aunt."

Jessica frowned. "Whatever your personal opinion of them, Echo, you really shouldn't ask me to share it."

She was sorry the moment the words were out. They had sounded censorious and schoolmarmish. As a guest here, it was no business of hers to teach Echo manners. She should simply have ignored the remark.

Echo went slightly red, and for a moment Jessica thought she was going to give an angry retort. Then, plainly making an effort, she swallowed. "Sorry, don't mind me. Can I get you a drink or something?"

Determined to make amends, Jessica answered effusively. "That's very sweet of you. But what I'm really dying for is a cup of coffee."

"Oh, sure. Okay, wait here." She turned away, saying as she did so: "I remember how you take it."

Jessica eyed her back thoughtfully. She was remembering the cigarette she had seen Echo smoking. Had the girl suspected her of recognizing it for what it was? And was she now ingratiating herself, in the hope of stopping Jessica reporting the incident to Morgana or Denton? Jessica smiled. She had firmly decided to say nothing of what she'd seen. But it wouldn't do the girl any harm to sweat for a bit.

A moment later Echo returned with coffee. "Oh, thank you, my dear. You've saved my life." Jessica sipped gratefully at the steaming cup. The girl stood by a little awkwardly. She seemed unable to make small talk. Then she glanced up, over Jessica's shoulder, muttered, "Excuse me," and edged away.

The next second Jessica realized that it was the approach of Denton that had driven her off. He came up, beaming. "Good morning, Jessica. Enjoying yourself? Quite an occasion, isn't it?"

"Yes, it is. In more ways than one. May I give you my very best wishes on your birthday?"

"You may indeed."

"Abby says that's *all* I'm allowed to give."

"Correct. Some people wanted to make quite a thing of this—birthday cake, even a kind of presentation. But I put my foot down. At my age a birthday isn't anything to be particularly proud of. Or to be ashamed of either, of course. I told everybody I'd accept their good wishes privately, but if they gave me anything more substantial, or tried to make a formal speech, I'd turf them out." He chuckled. "I usually get my own way."

"I'm sure you do," Jessica replied.

"That's coffee you're drinking? How about some punch?"

"No, thank you. This'll be fine. As a matter of fact, I hadn't realized a hunt breakfast required so much of the other kind of liquid refreshment."

He gave a grunt. "Only way to get most of these milksops over the first fence." He took her by the elbow. "Come on, my dear. At least let's get you something to eat."

No more than fifteen minutes later the imposing figure of the Master of the Hunt strode in through the big double doors and announced stentorianly: "Ladies and gentlemen—to horse!"

There was an immediate movement. Jessica's heart sank a little. This was it. She just hoped she didn't make too big a fool of herself. She emptied the glass of punch, with which Denton had eventually persuaded her to finish off her breakfast, and followed the crowd outside.

She saw Abby, who was already mounted, and who beckoned and pointed to where a stable boy was holding the already saddled Doughnut. Jessica walked across and, aided by a leg-up from the boy, got into the saddle with greater ease than she would have thought possible a few days previously. She walked Doughnut across toward Abby, but had to rein in sharply as a riderless horse veered across her path. Then she saw that Trish was clinging to the animal's bridle. She was red-faced and muttering angrily to herself as she tried to control it. "Keep still, damn you!" she hissed.

She took a grab at the saddle with one hand and started to raise her left foot to the stirrup. Again the horse, sensing something wrong with the rider, blundered sideways and Trish nearly fell.

Abby slipped from her saddle, handed her reins to a bystander and ran across. She grabbed the bridle of Trish's mount. As she patted and soothed the beast, she said calmly, "You know, you shouldn't be riding in your condition. It's dangerous to the horse."

Trish ignored this. With Abby holding the horse's head, she made a great effort and managed to lift herself into the saddle.

Abby tried once more. "Trish, look, why don't you think again? It's—"

Trish shot her a dirty look. "Oh, clear off! Go kiss up to father—while you've got the chance."

Abby's mouth dropped indignantly. "Because the day he goes, honey," Trish continued bitingly, "so do you!" She emphasized the last words with three pokes toward Abby with her riding crop. Then, giving a vicious jerk on the reins, she virtually pulled the horse's head from Abby's grasp, spun it around, kicked her heels into its sides and cantered off, scattering people and dogs before her.

Abby stood staring after her, her face white. Then she strode back to her own horse and remounted. Jessica rode up to her. "Ignore her, my dear," she said quietly.

Abby looked at her. "You know, Jess, around here all the *real* beasts walk on two legs."

Before Jessica could reply Denton trotted up. He was on his regular mount, a steady and reliable old gray called Sawdust. Teddy, keeping himself aloof from the main pack of hounds, was frisking around the horse's feet.

"All ready, Jessica?" Denton asked.

"As ready as I'll ever be, Denton."

"I'll stick close to you."

"Oh no, I'll be at the rear. I'm sure you'll want to go ahead."

"There's no way I'll persuade this old nag to keep up with the pack. He hasn't broken out of a trot for years."

The Master of the Hunt came up to them. "We're ready to move, Denton."

"Right." Denton walked Sawdust over to an intercom mounted on a post near the front steps. He spoke into it. "Barnes? We're ready to go. Open the gate."

There was a momentary crackle, then the security guard's voice was heard. "Very good, sir."

The hunt set off down the drive.

Jessica soon found herself enjoying the ride very much. It was a glorious day. Doughnut was in fine fettle, and with Denton riding one side of her and Abby the other—ready to help in case of emergency—Jessica never felt in the slightest danger. Moreover, they were soon so far behind the pack and the leading riders that there was fortunately no possibility of her being in on the kill.

She did, however, feel a bit guilty about holding Abby back. Her cousin was a superb horsewoman and ought to have been leading the field. At last she said as much. Denton backed her up.

"Yes, catch up with the leaders, Abby. And, Jessica, I suspect you're holding yourself back, too. Why don't you both go ahead? It can't be much fun poking along with an old man."

"I assure you," Jessica said, "I am perfectly happy just where I am."

"And I wish you'd stop calling yourself old, Denton," Abby put in. "In every way that matters you are in your prime."

"Thank you, my dear. Ah, if I were thirty years younger . . ." He winked at Jessica as he spoke, but she could tell he was pleased.

At that moment they heard galloping hooves from behind, and a second later Echo flashed past them. They'd come upon her, dismounted and tightening a girth, some minutes before, and now she was obviously intent on catching the pack. Her face was flushed and her eyes sparkling. She raised a hand in salute as she came level, but she didn't pause or speak.

Denton gave a grunt as Echo drew ahead. "That granddaughter of mine looks almost normal—"

He never finished the sentence, for just then something seemed to come over Sawdust. It was as if the sight of Echo's horse had awakened in him some long-dormant instinct against being overtaken. He tossed his head and whinnied. His eyes rolled and his ears went back.

Denton said sharply, "Steady, boy!" He reached out a hand to stroke the animal's neck. But before he could do so, Sawdust launched into a gallop.

"Whoa!" Denton roared. He pulled on the reins. But the horse took no notice. He had the bit between his teeth and was going like a champion three-year-old. Teddy, who had stuck close to Denton from the start, gave a yelp of protest and chased after him.

Abby uttered a gasp. "What's come over him?" She

gave her own mount a tap with her crop and set off in pursuit. Jessica took a deep breath, gave Doughnut a gentle kick, and the old mare broke into a lumbering canter. But she had no chance of catching up and Jessica was a fairly distant spectator of what ensued.

Sawdust was already rapidly closing on Echo's horse. The girl heard his hoofbeats, looked over her shoulder and then in amazement saw her grandfather shoot past.

Abby was only thirty yards behind. "What's he playing at?" Echo yelled to her. "Is he crazy?"

Abby didn't answer. She drew level, then overtook the girl. But she was making no inroad into Denton's lead.

At the far side of the field they were crossing was a stone wall, over six feet high. For a moment Abby was relieved at the sight of it, for it would surely bring Sawdust to a halt. She waited for the horse to slow. It was now less than forty yards from the wall. Still Sawdust was at full gallop. Thirty yards. Twenty. Abby's heart gave a leap of horror as she suddenly realized the horse was going to jump it.

It seemed that Denton had given up trying to stop the old gray. He was bending forward over his head, in the manner of one whispering encouragement to his mount.

Man and horse reached the wall. Sawdust gave a magnificent jump. He soared up—up—up. As he cleared it, with an inch to spare, Denton's voice rang out in a cry of triumph.

"Tallyho!"

Then he disappeared from Abby's sight. There came a horrible dull thud, and the sound of receding hoofbeats. But now they sounded different—lighter, as though the horse had been relieved of a burden.

Abby galloped up to the wall and reined in sharply. Fear at what she might see held her heart in an icy grip. She forced herself to edge her mount close to the wall and peer over. Then her stomach lurched. Denton Langley was sprawled on his back on the grass. He wasn't moving and his head was lying at an unnatural angle to his body.

Teddy, who had somehow found a way over or through the wall, was licking his face and whining.

For what seemed a long, long time—but was in fact only seconds—Abby just sat numbly staring down. Then she was recalled to her senses by the sound of hooves as Echo came thundering up. Her face was white.

Abby spun around and held up her hand. "Stay there, Echo!"

The girl whispered, "Grandfather—is he. . . ?"

Abby just shook her head. Then, without getting down from her horse, she pulled herself directly on to the top of the wall and dropped down onto the grass on the far side. She knelt down by the inert figure, gently pushed the agitated and bewildered Teddy aside and felt Denton's heart. She was just getting heavily to her feet when Jessica's face appeared over the wall.

Their eyes met. Abby slowly shook her head.

"Oh no . . ." Jessica's voice was a whisper.

Abby clambered back over the wall. She looked up at Echo. "I'm afraid he's dead, my dear."

Echo's face was bewildered. She seemed unable to comprehend what had happened. It was, Jessica thought, probably the first time she had come in contact with violent—or perhaps any—death.

"Can't—can't we do anything?" Echo sounded suddenly like a very young child.

"Yes, you can." Jessica spoke briskly. "Ride back to the house and tell them what's happened. Get them to send for an ambulance. Are you up to breaking the news to your mother?"

The girl nodded silently.

Abby said suddenly, "Get somebody to call the sheriff as well, Echo."

There was something so strange about her voice that Jessica glanced at her sharply. But Echo didn't seem to notice anything different. She just said wonderingly, "He was really enjoying that last gallop. When he passed by me he was—he was laughing."

Then she abruptly wheeled her horse and galloped off like the wind.

Jessica and Abby were left. Abby's face was very white, and for a moment Jessica thought she was going to faint. She wished she had some brandy or whiskey, but the best she could do was say: "Abby, why don't you sit down? Come along, lean up against the wall."

She took her cousin's arm, but Abby shook it off. "I'm all right, Jess."

"As you wish." She paused before adding: "Abby, I'm so terribly sorry. I know how you felt about him."

Abby looked at her. There were tears in her eyes. "He was a wonderful man, Jess. I—I admired him so much."

"I know."

"And he was so unhappy underneath all the jollity and charm. Because of *them*."

Jessica didn't need to ask whom she meant by *them*. Groping for words of comfort, she said, "Still, there are many worse ways to go. He died quickly and without lingering pain, doing what he liked to do best. He was enjoying himself: you heard what Echo said."

Abby nodded. "Of course—once he knew it was inevitable, he'd make the best of it. As soon as he realized that, whatever he did, Sawdust *was* going to take this wall— then he stopped trying to rein him in, but gave him every encouragement. It was brilliant. And I daresay he did relish the challenge of the jump—even though he must have known that he faced a terrible spill."

She took a handkerchief from the pocket of her jodhpurs and blew her nose hard.

Jessica said, "Abby, what made Sawdust take off like that? I thought he was so reliable."

"He was. He *is*. He will be again—if he hasn't injured himself and we get him back safely." She paused. "Once he gets the drug out of his system."

Jessica let her breath out slowly. "You're suggesting the horse was deliberately interfered with?"

"Yes."

"But, my dear, are you sure? I mean, couldn't it have been some sort of fit?"

Abby shook her head. "I've spent all my life around horses, Jess. I've never seen or heard of any natural cause that would have that effect. Just think of the speed he was going! I wouldn't have believed it possible. But I do know there are drugs that can have the most incredible effects. Normally, of course, they're given in small doses—just to improve an animal's form slightly, without it showing too much. But if a really big dose were given . . ." She trailed off.

"Abby, you know what you're suggesting is murder?" Jessica's voice was grave.

"Of course. Denton was an extremely rich man, Jess. He was also extremely fit. I believe his father lived to well over ninety. There was no reason why he shouldn't have done the same."

Her voice suddenly broke. "If—if it hadn't been for those greedy murdering swine." And she burst into tears.

Jessica put her arm around her. She didn't really know what to say.

Chapter Fourteen

A KNOCK came at the door of Abby's cottage. Jessica went to answer it. A tall, rather gangling, fair-haired young man was standing outside. He tipped his hat.

"Afternoon, Miss Fletcher."

"Oh, good afternoon, Mr. Roxie. Do come in."

She'd met Will Roxie shortly after Denton's death and had taken to him immediately. He was slow-spoken and friendly, seemingly more like a farm boy than a law officer. Though she suspected he was considerably shrewder than he seemed on the surface.

She wished she could have felt the same about the sheriff, Gus Millard, a burly, bull-necked, red-faced man who gave every indication of being even less shrewd than he looked.

She led the way into the living room. "Abby, it's the deputy."

Abby came in from the kitchen. "Oh, hello, Will."

"Miss Freestone, thought I'd drop by and let you know we've received the vet's report on those tests you wanted us to do on Sawdust."

"And?"

"Negative."

She made a gesture of irritation. "Predictable. It was hours before they found him. Besides, there *are* drugs that leave no trace."

Will shrugged. "Maybe. But there's no evidence they were used in this case."

"Will, the horse bolted like a mad thing, straight at that wall. Yet now he's perfectly normal—go and see him. How do you account for that—unless he was drugged?"

"Maybe you were mistaken, Miss Freestone."

She stiffened. "What do you mean?"

"Suppose he didn't bolt? Suppose it was Mr. Langley had a rush of blood to the head? Maybe he got fed up with plodding along at the back of the field and decided to jump that wall."

"Oh, nonsense!"

"Miss Echo says he was laughing when he passed her. *You* said he called out *tallyho* as he took the jump."

"I'm not saying he wasn't enjoying himself by then. But first of all, he was startled. He tried to stop the horse. It wouldn't stop. Yet there'd been nothing to spook it. And it's one of the quietest and most reliable animals in the stables."

He shrugged again. "Well, I don't say you're not right. There's just no proof. So that's it."

"What does that mean, exactly? No further investigation?"

"Afraid not. Sheriff says it goes down as an accident. Of course, there'll be an inquest. But we won't be putting forward any evidence to suggest foul play. Sorry."

Abby uttered an explosive noise that sounded like *tscha!* Then: "He was murdered," she said.

"Bring us some evidence, Miss Abby, and we'll investigate it. *I'd* be pleased to. But with nothing to go on . . ." He didn't finish the sentence.

After Will had left, Abby sat down wearily. "It's all wrong, Jess. One of those three's getting away with murder."

Jessica didn't answer. Abby looked at her sharply. "You do agree? You saw the way that horse behaved."

"Oh yes."

"Then one of them must have done it. Perhaps all of them."

"*Must* is a strong word, Abby. I wouldn't want to commit myself to it yet. I agree it does look highly suspicious."

Abby suddenly reached out and put a hand on Jessica's arm.

131

"Jess—you investigate it!"

"Oh my dear, I couldn't possibly!"

"But why not? You've done it before."

"In those cases the circumstances were quite different. Either somebody I knew, a friend or relative, was a suspect. Or I was myself. Or I was asked by the police to help. Nothing like that applies here. I have no standing, no opportunity to investigate, nothing to go on—aside from your belief that Sawdust was doped. What would I do? Where would I start?"

"Talk to them."

"Who? The family? My dear, I'm *your* guest. Denton made me welcome up at the house. They haven't—and they're not about to. If I started snooping around, cross-examining them, they'd have me off this estate double-quick. You as well, I expect."

Abby slumped back in her chair. "They'll have me out anyway, as soon as they can legally do so."

"Not necessarily. Somebody's got to be in charge of the horses."

"Oh, they'll sell them off, for sure. None of them is really interested. Besides, I wouldn't want to work for a crook, a bitch, or a fool."

"I'm terribly sorry, my dear. You were so happy here."

"Oh well, all good things must come to an end. And I suppose I have a couple of weeks' grace, at least. We'll know the exact position after the reading of the will tomorrow. And you will stay on for a bit won't you?"

"Well, I was invited for a holiday."

"I know. It's just that there's not going to be much of a holiday atmosphere around the place. But I'd feel terrible on my own now."

"I'll stay as long as you want me to." She paused. "And Abby—if I get a chance to . . . well, talk, ask questions, find out things—then I'll do my best."

"Oh, thanks, Jess, that's super!"

"Now, it won't be what you call an investigation. Just conversation. So don't expect too much."

Chapter Fifteen

IN the living room at Langley Manor, the atmosphere was both tense and gloomy. Spenser stood by the mantelpiece, nervously taking long, deep pulls on his cigarette. At the coffee table Morgana was gazing fixedly into the bottom of a teacup. Echo was staring moodily out the window. Trish, at the bar, was pouring herself a vodka. Abby and Tom Cassidy sat side by side on the sofa. Her face was pale and drawn, while he just looked sad. The only utterly relaxed figure in the room was Teddy, who was fast asleep on the hearth rug. Nobody was talking.

Spenser suddenly threw his cigarette half-smoked into the fireplace and walked across to the bar. He pointed to his sister's vodka glass. "Add some orange juice, and you can call that breakfast."

Trish didn't seem to hear this. "Where's Boswell?" she said impatiently. She looked at her wristwatch. "He should have been here three minutes ago."

"Perhaps he's kindly postponing the evil hour for us."

"Don't be silly, Spense." She spoke sharply. "It's going to be all right."

He raised his eyebrows. "Wish I was so confident."

"Oh dear. Oh my."

They turned to see Morgana stumbling toward them. She was carrying the teacup and was positively trembling.

Spenser gave a sigh. "What now, Morgana?"

She thrust the cup toward them. "The tea leaves! Look!"

They glanced into it. "So?" Trish said in a bored voice.

133

"But don't you see?"

"See *what*? Oh, Morgana—"

It was at that moment the front door bell chimed. Instantly every head swung to face the big double doors. Half a minute passed before they opened and the butler announced: "Mr. Boswell."

Marcus Boswell bustled into the room. He was wearing a suit of English tweed and was carrying a briefcase. He crossed to Spenser, holding out his hand.

"Spenser, please accept my heartfelt sympathy. This place won't be the same without Denton Langley."

"Thank you, Marcus. We are devastated by our loss."

Boswell made as if to shake hands with Trish and Morgana; met Trish's cool glare and Morgana's distant, troubled gaze, thought better of it, and gave a series of hurried nods to include everyone in the room. He cleared his throat nervously and said, "Ah . . . yes. Well, as Denton's attorney, I'd best get down to business."

"What a brilliant idea," Trish drawled.

Boswell flushed slightly. He put his briefcase on the table, opened it, and to everyone's surprise drew from it a videocassette.

"What's this?" Trish asked. "Home movies?"

"No, Trish, it's the latest in will technology."

"You mean *that* is father's will?" Spenser pointed to the cassette.

"In a sense. Not his legal will, of course—that's all down in written form." Boswell tapped the briefcase. Then he held up the cassette. "This is Denton's message to you all, in which he explains his testamentary dispositions. He recorded it just over a month ago."

"A voice from beyond the grave." Morgana spoke in hollow tones.

"Exactly. So, if I may. . . ?"

"Go ahead," Spenser told him.

Boswell crossed to the television set, switched it on, inserted the cassette into the VCR that stood next to it and pressed the Play button.

The screen flickered into life—and there before them

was Denton Langley. Trish drew her breath in sharply, Morgana gave a little moan, Spenser muttered something. Tom Cassidy and Abby leaned forward in their seats.

Denton had been photographed sitting in his favorite chair. He looked relaxed and happy. One hand was holding a brandy glass; the other rested on the head of Teddy— the dog was draped over the arm of the chair. Denton raised the glass and smiled into the camera.

"Greetings, friends and kinfolk. I went to a lot of trouble getting this little show together for you all. Hope you enjoy it."

At the sound of Denton's voice, Teddy had sat up. He was staring at the screen, his head to one side. He was plainly puzzled. Abby momentarily wondered how far, with no sense of smell to guide him, he was able to recognize the image on the screen as his master. And what did he make of the strange dog sitting by him? Then she concentrated on the television screen.

"Since I know you're all there, waiting breathlessly," Denton said, "I think I'll prolong the suspense with a parting word to each of you. Spenser—it's too bad they keep blowing up your clients. But I never thought lobbying for Arab dictators was a decent job for you." He paused. "But then, what would be? I've never figured out an answer to that one."

Abby glanced at Spenser. His jaw had tightened, but otherwise he displayed no reaction at all.

"As for you, baby Trish," Denton went on, "you always were your mother's spoiled child. I'm glad she can't see you now—guzzling martinis the way you used to suck up root beer, and collecting men instead of dolls. Find a nicer hobby, honey. This one's not only unseemly. It's dangerous."

Abby cast a quick glance at Trish. The girl had gone pale and was chewing at her lip. Denton had stopped to take a sip of brandy. Now he resumed.

"Morgana. You're not a bad woman. But you've got no common sense. Come out of that fantasy world and face your problems."

Morgana was smiling gently and beatifically at the screen.

"Because you do have problems, you know," Denton continued. "Such as that mixed-up daughter of yours. Suggest you pay a bit more heed to her. She could use it."

He smiled. "You there, Echo? I expect so. Is there anything stirring under that unique haircut of yours?"

"You'll never know, old man," Echo said loudly.

Denton shifted slightly in his chair. "Well, so much for fond farewells. Now to business. Boswell's got the usual 'sound mind' claptrap written down someplace. So—this is how it goes. There are some charitable donations that I won't go into now, also small bequests to various distant relatives and old friends, such as Robert Hawkins, my broker, who won't be here when this is played. There's a cash gift for each of the staff, and Barnes gets something extra for guarding the paintings. Now, here's the part you all came for. I'm sure my old friend Tom is watching. Tom—you get my shotguns and all my fishing tackle. Enjoy 'em—and mind you look after 'em."

Tom Cassidy blew his nose suddenly, but Abby hardly noticed, for she heard her own name.

"Abby, my dear, you've trained practically every animal on the place. In a few months I figure you'll have my Guernseys jumping through hoops. You've done wonders with the horses. I want you to have one. Any one. It's your choice. If you take my advice, you'll pick Silver King; but it's up to you."

Abby gave a gasp of amazement. Her face was a study of delight. Then she suddenly felt tears pricking at the back of her eyes and raised her hands to her face. She had to force herself to concentrate as Denton's image continued: "Next, the paintings—the art collection, as Marcus insists on calling them. They're going to the National Gallery."

Simultaneously, exclamations of horror came from Spenser and Trish. Denton, with perfect anticipation of their reaction, was nodding. "That's right, children. A fast three million in oils—on their way to Washington. As for the rest of my estate, built with my brains and my sweat, it comes to about fifteen million dollars. It takes a sound mind and good judgment to handle that much money. Maybe even a good nature. So, who meets those requirements?''

There was a breathless hush in the room. Nobody stirred. Trish was biting her nails. Slowly Denton shook his head.

''Sorry, children, none of you do. I therefore leave you the sum of fifty thousand dollars each. The remainder I bequeath''—Denton paused and looked down—''to my faithful companion, Teddy. Goodbye, folks.''

The camera zoomed in on the head of the dog and the screen went blank.

For an instant there was a stunned silence in the room. It was broken by the principal beneficiary, who, hearing his name spoken, uttered an enquiring: ''Woof!''

The next moment the room broke into a medley of sound. Denton's family turned on Boswell in fury. They all talked at once. Trish grabbed his arm. Abby could pick out odd sentences.

''Of all the dirty tricks!''

''This is insane! Teddy's a *dog*!''

''I may faint.''

''Boswell, we'll break that will.''

This last was Spenser, and here Boswell managed to get a word in.

''You'd be advised not to try it, Spenser. It includes a clause stipulating that, if you challenge it, you're cut out completely.''

''Marcus.'' Trish spoke in a voice of low venom. ''I'll never forgive you for what you've done. I'm warning you—I'm going to get even.''

''I was only carrying out your father's instructions, Trish.''

Spenser was staring malevolently at Teddy. Boswell seemed to read his thoughts. ''And don't even think of harming that animal. If he dies of anything but natural causes, every dime goes to the ASPCA.''

''Well, well, well,'' Jessica said slowly, ''how very remarkable.''

Abby hugged herself. ''Isn't it gorgeous? Oh, Jess, you

should have seen their faces! Trish seems to blame poor old Marcus. Never forgive him, going to get even, and so on."

"And what's your position now, Abby?"

"Well, I'm employed by Teddy! But, of course, Marcus Boswell is trustee or executor or administrator, or whatever it's called. He made it quite clear he wants me to stay on."

"That's marvelous. And you've got a fine horse of your own in the bargain. I suppose you *will* choose Silver King?"

"You bet! I introduced you to him, didn't I?"

"I think it would be more accurate to say you presented me to him. I felt from your buildup I ought to curtsy."

"Sorry. But really, Jess, he is the most magnificent beast! A potential Olympic champion. Never did I dream of owning such a horse. You know, one day I laid out the toughest treble I could devise: it consisted of a—"

Jessica gently interrupted. "Yes, my dear, you told me. And at the moment I'm really more interested in *you*. Do you think you're going to be happy here, under the circumstances? Feeling as you do about the Langleys? And as they feel about you? Wouldn't it perhaps be better just to take Silver King and go?"

Abby shook her head decisively. "Oh, no. I'm not leaving here until I—until *we*—get to the bottom of Denton's death. That's the beauty of the new situation. We can make whatever inquiries we like. There's not a thing they can do about it."

She leaned back in her chair and clasped her hands behind her head. "You know, Jess, I think I'm going to enjoy myself in the days to come." She smiled a contented smile.

But Jessica wasn't smiling. She had promised to help Abby. But *she* anticipated no enjoyment in what lay ahead. She suspected that Abby, in the hope of arriving at the truth, was going deliberately to needle Denton's family. Which could lead to a very nasty situation at Langley Manor in the not too distant future.

Chapter Sixteen

THE trouble Jessica had anticipated began the very next day. She and Abby were sitting in the sun after breakfast reading their papers when there came a whinny from the stable yard. It was followed by the sound of hooves on concrete.

Abby dropped her paper and got suddenly to her feet. "What's going on?" she exclaimed. And she hurried off in the direction of the sound.

Jessica hastily followed, and was on Abby's heels when she entered the yard. They saw Trish in the act of saddling up a chestnut gelding that Jessica knew her cousin had been intending to put through his paces that morning. Abby marched angrily over to the girl.

"Just who gave you permission to take that animal from his stall?" she demanded.

Trish gazed at her coolly. "I gave myself permission."

"Well, you can just put him back."

"I shall do no such thing."

Abby stepped closer. "I would remind you that I am in charge of these stables. Nobody takes out a horse without my permission. Especially not you."

An expression of fury came over Trish's face. "Now listen, Miss Stable Nanny, *I* would remind *you* that you are an employee of this estate. A servant."

"And you aren't even that. You don't own this estate. You have no rights here at all."

"Well, we're here—Spense, Morgana and I—and we're

139

staying. Marcus Boswell had sense enough not to try and cheat us out of our family home. So you'll have to get used to our being around.''

"And you'll have to get used to *my* being around. Just remember that these stables are my domain—officially.''

Trish sneered. "For the time being, maybe. Just until we get this crazy will overturned. Spense has already been in touch with a lawyer from D.C. who specializes in these cases. He's flying down to see us very soon.''

Abby regarded her contemptuously. "Never give up, do you? Your first scheme to get your hands on your father's money failed, so—''

Trish interrupted. "Just what do you mean by that?''

"You know very well what I mean.'' Abby was shouting now.

Jessica touched her gently on the arm. "Abby, I think perhaps enough has been said.''

"No!'' It was Trish's turn to shout. "Let's have this out. I know you—both of you—have been going around saying Sawdust was doped. It's pretty obvious what you're implying. Well, I warn you: it can be very dangerous to make accusations of that sort.''

"Is that a threat?''

"Take it any way you like.''

A voice called urgently: "Trish!''

It was Spenser. He was striding toward them, an angry expression on his face. "For heaven's sake,'' he snapped. "You can be heard halfway across the estate.''

Trish swung around to him. "She's just accused me of murdering Father.''

Spenser stared. "Is that true, Miss Freestone?''

"No.''

Trish gave a gasp. "Why, you lying—''

Abby cut in. "I didn't accuse your sister *personally*, Mr. Langley. I say *somebody* murdered your father. Somebody who had a good motive. Or believed he had.''

Spencer when white. "Meaning me?'' he asked very quietly.

Abby shrugged. "I repeat: I make no personal accusations."

Spenser struggled to control his temper. He took several deep breaths before replying: "I would be careful what you say, Miss Freestone. Very careful."

"Don't worry about me, Mr. Langley. But thanks for the warning."

Trish said suddenly, "Oh, come on, Spense. She's not worth fighting with." She dropped the reins of the chestnut and strode off to the house.

Abby sighed. "Typical! Leaves me to put the horse back in his stall."

"Oh, here!" Spenser grabbed up the reins. "I'll do it."

"No, it's my job."

Abby reached out to take the reins from him. But Jessica decided it was time she intervened. She again took her cousin by the arm, more firmly this time.

"Let him do it, Abby."

"But—"

"Let him do it!" Jessica turned her and began to lead her, still resisting, back in the direction of her cottage, calling over her shoulder: "Thank you, Mr. Langley."

"Jess, really," Abby muttered, "there's no need—"

"There is every need. That had gone on quite long enough."

"You really *should* be careful, you know, Abby," said a voice.

They stopped. It was Morgana who had spoken. She was emerging from the shadow of an empty stall, though Jessica could not imagine how she had gotten there without being seen, unless she had been there since before the fracas started. She was wearing a long black dress covered with exotic emblems, and many strings of beads. She was shaking her head and giving her beatific, unearthly smile.

They both stared at her for a moment, then Abby pulled herself together. "I'm not afraid of Spenser," she said.

"I was thinking of Trish," Morgana said. "Her Gemini is in the ascendant, your Capricorn is at low ebb, and last night three owls were seen in a black oak tree."

Abby stared at her, hands on hips. "Do you really expect to frighten me with that gibberish?"

Morgana was unabashed. She shrugged. "The signs are there for the reading."

Before Abby could speak again, there suddenly came the terrified whinny of a horse from behind them. They spun around to see the chestnut, saddle askew, bolting out of his stall. At the same time they heard a ferocious growling and barking from inside the stall. Abby broke into a run, back the way they had come. Jessica and Morgana followed her.

Abby arrived at the stall and peered in to see Spenser backed into the corner, a terrified expression on his face. In one hand he held a bucket and in the other a riding crop, and with them he was trying to ward off a viciously snarling dog. It was Teddy. His teeth were bared, his hackles up. He was making aggressive little darts forward, trying to get at Spenser.

Abby gave an angry exclamation. "What have you been doing to that dog?"

Spenser threw her a furious glance. "Call the brute off!" he yelled.

Abby was about to respond angrily again, then thought better of it and addressed the dog in a special high-pitched command voice that she used on animals.

"Teddy! Good boy! Down, Teddy! Sit!"

The dog glanced up at her and whined. For a moment it seemed he was going to disobey, but then he backed away from Spenser and settled down on his haunches.

Spenser dropped the bucket and strode out of the stall. His face was red with fury and embarrassment. He positively snarled, himself, as he addressed Jessica and Morgana.

"That damn dog has got to be destroyed!"

Morgana gasped. "Spenser, what happened?"

"He just started attacking me—the vicious brute."

Abby came out of the stall. Teddy, head lowered, panting and looking chastened and very tired, was at her heels. "You must have done something to provoke him," Abby said calmly.

"I did no such thing!" Spenser shouted. "I didn't even know the crazy creature was there until I heard him snarling behind me. I was concentrating on the horse. The dog obviously hates me."

Abby calmly bent and tickled Teddy's ears. "Yes, he's a sensible animal."

"Now, look here—" Spenser burst out, but Abby interrupted sharply.

"Did he bite you?"

"N-no." The admission came almost reluctantly. "But he damn well would have if I'd given him the chance."

"What about the horse?" Abby was still bending over the dog. Her hand was fingering his collar.

"Oh, no," Spenser sneered, "you wouldn't train him to attack one of your precious horses. Only me."

Abby ignored the gibe. "What's the matter, Abby?" Jessica asked.

Abby looked up. Her face was troubled. "There's blood on his collar."

"You see!" Spenser's voice was triumphant. "I knew it! The animal's dangerous. He'll have to go."

At that moment Teddy slumped down onto his side and closed his eyes. Abby knelt down by him and felt his heart. Then she put both hands under his body and effortlessly got to her feet, the dog in her arms. Teddy lay limp and unresisting.

Spenser's eyes lit up. "Is he—is he dead?"

"No such luck, Spenser. He's been drugged. I'm taking him to the vet. Jess, will you drive?"

"Yes, of course." Jessica hurried ahead to the car and opened the doors.

Abby spoke over her shoulder. "Better finish the job, Spense. Catch that horse and put him away. He probably doesn't like you either, but try not to cry about it."

"So you were right," Jessica said thoughtfully.

"I was never in any doubt," Abby said.

They were on their way home from the vet's, Abby now

at the wheel; Teddy, still exhausted, stretched out in the back.

"What did the vet say the stuff was called?"

"Search me. I'm only interested in its effects. Jess, who'd want to do that to Teddy? I can understand them wanting to poison him—if it wasn't for that clause in the will. But what's the point in drugging him? It's obvious why they did it to Sawdust."

"The vet said he found no trace of that substance in the horse."

"So, he made a mistake or they used different stuff. Sawdust was drugged—to kill Denton. But whom did they expect Teddy to kill? *Me*? Did it backfire on them when he attacked Spenser instead?"

Jessica shook her head. "No, I don't think that was the plan. I don't believe your life is in danger. Not at the moment."

"Then why? Do you have any ideas?"

"I have a vague idea of what somebody may be up to. But I'm not sure it would work. It would depend on the exact wording of Denton's will."

"What do you mean?"

"Well, suppose Teddy were destroyed officially—by order of the court? It wouldn't be strictly natural causes. But it wouldn't be the result of foul play against him either. So what would happen to his inheritance then?"

"You mean—they gave him something that would drive him to attack people, so that he'd be put to sleep without their laying a finger on him? Why, that's fiendish! You know, those people are absolute scum. Oh, wait till I see them again! I'll tear them off such a strip—"

"Abby, I think that would be very ill-advised."

"Why? You're not saying they're innocent, are you?"

"I'm saying that I cannot believe in a full-scale family conspiracy to kill their father. They're not *all* guilty."

"Then you find out who *is* the guilty one, and I'll apologize to the others."

Jessica sighed to herself. It seemed impossible to argue with her cousin in this mood.

Abby suddenly chuckled. "You know, the really delicious thing is Teddy turning and attacking Spenser. He knows who his real enemies are."

"I'm not so sure of that," Jessica said. "Remember the blood on his collar. It seems he did attack somebody else first."

"And I know who they're going to claim it was, too." Abby pointed through the windshield.

For the last minute or so they'd been traveling up the drive and had just turned into the stable yard. Parked in the middle was the sheriff's car. Standing near it were Millard, Spenser, and a scraggly, balding, middle-aged man wearing a tattered old checked shirt with the sleeves rolled up. His left arm was heavily bandaged, and he seemed to be remonstrating with Spenser while the sherrif tried to calm him down.

"Potts!" Abby muttered between her teeth: "I might have guessed!"

"Who is he?"

"He's a farmer. His place abuts the estate. He's a drunk, a liar, a cheat, and he treats his animals abominably."

She drew up near the three men. Potts immediately peered into the back of the car. Then he pointed at Teddy and turned to Millard.

"That's the dog, Sheriff. That's the dog that attacked me."

Abby and Jessica got out of the car. The sheriff tipped his hat. " 'Morning, ladies. I'm here on official business. Mr. Potts claims that there pooch bit him."

Abby regarded Potts coldly. "Do you have any witnesses?"

"Witnesses? What do I need witnesses for? Just take a look at my arm! Think I bit it myself?" Potts started trying to undo his bandage.

"There's no need for that," Spenser said. "No one's denying you were bitten."

"But what evidence is there that Teddy did it?" Abby demanded.

"Oh, for heaven's sake, Miss Freestone," Spenser said

irritably. "What's the point in denying it? You saw how the animal went for me."

"He didn't bite you."

"Understand there was blood on his collar, though, Miss Freestone," the sheriff put in.

Abby glared at Spenser. "Thank you very much, Mr. Langley. Determined to put the boot in, aren't you?"

Spenser shrugged. "Wouldn't be right to withhold information from the police."

Abby turned to Millard. "Sheriff, that blood on the collar could be anything. Teddy might have killed a rabbit or a rat."

"Our lab boys can easily find out, Miss Freestone."

"Oh, all right, take the collar and run your tests."

"I will, but I'm going to have to take the dog in, too. Reckon there's a *prima facie* case against him." He pronounced the Latin phrase carefully.

"Listen," said Abby, "we've just come from the vet's. He confirms Teddy was drugged with some stuff that would make him behave viciously. If Teddy did bite Potts, he couldn't help himself."

"Maybe so, Miss Freestone. But being under the influence of drink or drugs is no defense to a criminal charge—though it may be an extenuating circumstance when it comes to sentencing. Especially if the stuff was forcibly administered. However, that's a matter for the judge. Whatever the cause, the animal's dangerous. I gotta put him where he can't do any harm. So I'd be obliged if you'd move him into the back of my vehicle."

"I'll ride to town with him," Abby said with resignation. "He has to know he's got one friend." She turned to Jessica. "Jess, will you ring Marcus Boswell? Tell him what's happened and ask him to put the wheels in motion to get Teddy sprung as quickly as possible."

Jessica nodded. "I can't imagine he'll need much persuading. After all, I don't suppose he has many millionaire clients, and it must be extremely rare for one of them to be arrested. Particularly for biting somebody."

Chapter Seventeen

IT was after lunch the next day that the phone rang in the cottage. Abby answered it.

"Abby?"

She recognized the voice. "Yes, Mr. Boswell."

"Well, it's taken my entire bag of legal tricks, but I've arranged to have Teddy released on his own recognizance."

"Oh, that's marvelous!"

"I'd like to have you look after him most of the time from now on. Okay?"

"Yes, of course—great."

"Good. And times when you can't keep an eye on him, I suggest you put him in Barnes' care. He's a reliable man."

"Will do."

"In fact, it might be an idea to let him or his assistant have the dog in the security room at night. No one can get into it from outside, so he'd be perfectly safe there and you could relax."

"Good idea," said Abby.

"Then that's settled. You can pick up Teddy at the sheriff's office as soon as you like."

"I'll get down there right away."

"Now, Abby, I'm afraid that *was* human blood on Teddy's collar—same type as Potts'. So for heaven's sake make sure he stays out of trouble from now on in. If anything like this should happen again . . ." He left the sentence unfinished.

"I'll take good care of him."

"I'm sure you will. Oh, by the way, you'll be happy to know he wasn't rabid."

"Are they sure?"

Boswell laughed. "Positive. Potts hasn't died." He hung up.

Abby put down the receiver.

"Good news?" Jessica asked.

"Very. Teddy's coming home." She relayed all that she had been told. "I'm going to collect him now. Coming?"

Jessica nodded. "I'll get my coat."

It was after they had picked up an ecstatic, and completely recovered, Teddy from a reluctant sheriff and were on their way back to the car when Abby suddenly stopped and touched Jessica on the arm. "Enemy sighted." She pointed.

Jessica looked across the street and saw, emerging from an office building, Spenser, Trish and Morgana. Accompanying them was a tall, sleek, prosperous-looking man in a dark business suit.

"The lawyer from D.C., do you suppose?" Abby murmured.

"I wouldn't be a bit surprised."

"Marcus Boswell has his offices in that building. Shall we try and find out what's been going on?"

"Oh, do you think we should interfere?"

"Surely, as Teddy's official guardian, I have a right to know if there's any chance of him losing his inheritance. Come on."

Gripping Teddy's lead firmly, she started purposefully across the street. Jessica hesitated for a moment, then followed.

Marcus Boswell's suite of offices was luxuriously equipped with oak paneling and real leather furniture. Obviously valuable antiques abounded. The receptionist announced Jessica and Abby over the intercom and they heard Boswell say: "Oh, send them right in."

He met them at the door of his private office. "Ladies, do come in. I see the prisoner's been released."

At that moment the phone rang. The receptionist answered it, listened, covered the mouthpiece and said, "Bob Hawkins. Third time he's called today."

"Tell him I'm tied up."

Boswell ushered Jessica and Abby through the door, closed it and ensconced them in deep and very comfortable chairs. Teddy lay down on the thick carpet and went immediately to sleep.

Boswell sat behind a massive oak desk and regarded them benignly. "To what do I owe this pleasure?"

"Sheer nosiness, I'm afraid," Abby said. "We saw the Langleys leaving."

"Oh."

"That man with them: Trish said they were consulting a big-shot lawyer from Washington. Was that him?"

Boswell nodded slowly. "One Gary Deems. His specialty is breaking wills."

"Can they do that?"

"They can try."

"But what about that clause, cutting them out completely if they do?"

"Well, you know, a well-drawn will can stand up to fire, famine and pestilence. Denton's was well drawn, but it's always possible to find some loophole."

"And Mr. Deems has found one?" Jessica inquired.

"More like a rathole," Boswell said.

"Can we know what it is?" asked Abby. "I *am* an interested party."

"I don't see why not. We're all on the same side, after all. Well, Deems' angle is the question of sound mind."

Abby gave a snort of derision. "Nonsense! Denton Langley's mind was as sound as a bell!"

Boswell shook his head. "You misunderstand me. He's not thinking of Langley's mind."

Abby frowned. "Then whose. . . ?"

For answer, Boswell pointed down at the sleeping dog on the carpet.

"Teddy!" Abby gasped. Without waking, the dog wagged his tail.

Boswell nodded. "If a court were to declare the dog mentally incompetent—"

"But that's ridiculous!"

"I know it is. But it might take a lot of years in court to prove it. For instance, if a dog had a reputation for attacking people, would that be evidence of insanity?"

Abby glanced at Jessica. "Now we know why he was fed that dope."

Boswell raised a hand. "Abby, you must watch it. It's safe enough to say that sort of thing in your lawyer's office; but get in the habit of saying it, and you may find yourself in court."

"I know. But it's all so beastly! I hate to think of those people getting their hands on Denton's estate, after all."

"Now, don't worry. I may be a country boy, but I know a few legal tricks myself."

At that moment the intercom on his desk buzzed. He sighed. "Excuse me, ladies."

The voice of the receptionist said, "I'm sorry, Mr. Boswell, but it's Bob Hawkins again. Says it's vital he speak to you."

"Okay, put him on." He addressed the women. "Sorry, ladies, seems I just have to take this call."

"We must go," said Jessica.

She got to her feet, and Abby followed suit. "Thanks for your time, Mr. Boswell." She gave a tug on Teddy's lead, and he jumped up eagerly.

"Anytime, Abby," Boswell told her. "Remember what I said—don't worry—and keep a sharp eye on that VIP— which stands for 'very important pooch.' "

Abby was silent driving home in the car, and responded to Jessica's remarks shortly. Jessica sensed that for some reason she wasn't at the moment on her cousin's good side. But it wasn't until they were back at the cottage and having a cup of tea that she plucked up courage to ask directly: "Abby, have I done anything to offend you?"

Abby looked at her. "No, certainly not."

"I'm glad."

"But to be quite frank, Jess, I'm rather disappointed you haven't done anything yet."

"Done anything?"

"About the case."

"Oh, Abby, what can I do? If the Langleys—or one of them—drugged Sawdust, the deed's over and done with. I don't see any way to prove it. The police might be able to trace the purchase of the drug to them, but there's no way I can."

"I know that. But you did say you'd try to help."

"I was thinking of conversation. I do have a sort of knack for drawing people out. And then I sometimes get an idea. But the way your relationship with the Langleys has deteriorated makes conversation of that kind with them impossible. You call them the enemy; no doubt that's how they think of you. And from their point of view, I'm firmly in the enemy camp. So just tell me, what *can* I do?"

Abby sighed. "Oh, I don't know. Sorry, Jess. I suppose I'm being unreasonable. I was thinking of you as a miracle worker."

"Which I'm most definitely not."

"Well, perhaps it's a good thing, in a way. It means I'm on my own. I can plan my own campaign. And I don't have to be as cautious as you, or Marcus Boswell. I can be a little more drastic in my methods." There was a strange note in her voice.

"What do you mean, Abby?" Jessica spoke sharply.

"What?" Abby blinked. "Oh, nothing, Jess. I haven't got anything definite in mind. I was just thinking. More tea?"

Chapter Eighteen

SEVERAL days passed. By tacit consent, the topic of Denton Langley's death was dropped. Jessica spent her time reading, walking on the estate, doing a little gentle riding on Doughnut and planning the main outline of her next book. Abby was busy with the horses. She kept Teddy with her at most times, but on the occasions she was not able to watch him, she followed Boswell's suggestion and had Barnes look after him. The guard was clearly fond of him, and seemed pleased to have the dog's company at night.

Marcus Boswell visited regularly to check on his client's welfare, and himself took Teddy for several long walks.

Jessica and Abby saw little of the Langleys, who confined themselves mainly to the house. Twice, according to Barnes, Gary Deems called, and remained over an hour on each occasion.

For a while Jessica worried about her cousin. She'd seen a tremendous change come over her during the short period since Denton Langley's death. The cause was not hard to find. Abby had hero-worshiped her employer. He had been her benefactor, giving her the sort of position she had dreamed of all her life. Perhaps he had been a father figure to her. Perhaps, in spite of the difference in their ages, she had been—maybe unconsciously—in love with him. But then had come the tremendous shock of Denton's death. This had been followed by the discovery that he had remembered Abby so magnificently in his will. Her feeling of indebtedness had deepened still further. Linked with this had been the conviction—possibly, but by no means certainly, justified—that he had been murdered; and the growing suspicion that nobody else shared her conviction or was going to do anything about it.

However, her cousin's presence must have been a comfort. Given Jessica's reputation as a private detective, Abby had no doubt felt that she could have no better ally in her fight to establish the truth. But Jessica had let her down—or that, at least, was how Abby must have seen it. The famous solver of mysteries had failed even to investigate this one. When Jessica had at last pointed out the impossibility of taking action, Abby must have felt very much alone.

Jessica herself was highly conscious of the situation; she felt guilty about it. While her logic told her that everything she had said to her cousin was true, her conscience constantly nagged, telling her there was surely something she could do.

But much as she racked her brains, she couldn't think of anything.

However, as the day's passed, Abby's manner seemed gradually to return to normal. She brooded less, stopped giving forth streams of invective against the Langleys and talked no more about drastic methods. It was a relief to Jessica, who began to feel that when her vacation ended she would finally be able to go home with an easier mind about her cousin.

That, though, was before the second murder.

Chapter Nineteen

IT was one A.M. In the security room Barnes yawned. Four hours before Smedley would take over for him. This was the boring shift. Nothing ever happened.

He glanced down at Teddy, who was fast asleep in his basket. "Fine company you are tonight, pal," he said out loud.

Teddy gave a snore, but didn't wake up. Barnes grinned and glanced at his watch. Time to make some coffee.

He was just going to get to his feet when he saw movement and light on one of his monitors. He stared closely at the screen, which was the one that showed the area of the main gate. The headlamps of an approaching vehicle were illuminating the scene; and as Barnes watched, the car itself drew up just outside the gate. He couldn't see much detail, but it had surely halted in a queer position, as if one wheel had mounted the pavement; the lights were shining at an angle across the road. Barnes felt the stirrings of suspicion, and his hand inched toward the phone.

Then he relaxed as a human figure moved from the darkness into the glare of the headlights in front of the car—a figure wearing a full-length fur coat and a head scarf, and staggering slightly as it moved.

Barnes shook his head disgustedly. "Trish," he muttered. "Drunk again. I might have guessed!"

He saw the figure reach out to the intercom on the gatepost, and a second later a buzzer sounded loudly in the security room. It woke Teddy, who sat up with a jerk.

"Relax, feller," Barnes said. "It's no friend of yours."

He reached out and pressed a buttom marked MAIN GATE. On the screen he saw the gate start to roll back and the buzzer stopped. Teddy was now sitting up and staring at the screen with every indication of interest, ears cocked and head on one side.

"Go on, girl," Barnes muttered. "Get back in your car. The gate's open."

However, the next second he stiffened, as without warning the figure on the screen suddenly swayed, fell heavily onto the road and lay still.

Barnes groaned. "Passed out."

He got wearily to his feet. Teddy looked at him hopefully and gave a little yelp.

"Sorry, boy, no walks tonight. More than my job's worth to let you out."

He checked his gun, picked up a flashlight, walked to the door and opened it. Then he turned.

"Okay, Teddy, mind the store while I'm gone, okay?"

He went out, closed the door and carefully locked it with one of a bunch of keys that hung from his belt. Then he started walking briskly across the grass in the direction of the main gate.

It was a still, dark night, and the only sound to break the silence was the single call of a mockingbird, which rang out just as Barnes got his first direct sight of the main gate. The car lights were the only illumination, but by them he could see an inert human form still lying near the side of the drive.

The next second, Barnes stopped dead. He stared in amazement. The gate, which could be operated only from the security room, had started to move. It was closing.

He gave an exclamation. "Now, how in tarnation—"

The words died in his throat. With utter horror he had suddenly realized that Trish Langley was lying on the rails, directly in the path of the gate. Her head was just inches from the massive concrete gatepost.

Barnes broke into a run, at the same time yelling at the top of his voice:

"Miss Langley! Look out!"

The girl didn't move. Barnes continued to sprint and shout, but he was still forty yards from the gate when he realized that he was going to be too late.

The grinding of metal on metal was a sound that was to remain in Barnes' mind for years to come. So was the sight of the gate, inexorably closing, moving nearer and nearer to Trish Langley's head.

At the very last moment Barnes stopped running and shut his eyes. There was nothing to be gained by watching. He only wished he could have shut his ears to that final sound of Trish's head being driven up against the gatepost. . . .

Chapter Twenty

"**N**OW, let's get this straight," Sheriff Millard said. "You're saying the gate can only be closed from inside that security room of yours."

Barnes nodded vigorously. "The only way it can be closed electronically, yes. It can be hauled across manually in an emergency, of course, but it certainly wasn't closed manually tonight."

"And you say you locked the security room behind you when you left?"

"Sure did."

"And there was nobody there then?"

"Nope."

"How many keys are there?"

"I've only ever seen one. I hand it to Smedley when we change shift."

The sheriff stared at him belligerently. "Seems to me you're putting your own neck in a noose. You're saying no outsider got into the security room, yet someone pressed the button. We only got your word the gate started to close when you were on the drive. What's to have stopped you closing the gate on Miss Langley before you left the room?"

Barnes' face went red. "Why, you great—"

Marcus Boswell, whom Barnes had telephoned soon after finding the body, and who had driven straight over, laid a restraining hand on his arm. "That's ridiculous,

Sheriff. What motive could Barnes have had for murdering Trish?''

''You never know what sort of motives are going to come to light till you start digging.''

''Look, if Barnes was guilty, it would be easy for him to say he forgot to lock the security-room door, so somebody could have gotten in and pressed the button. But he didn't. He's told you the truth.''

Millard scratched his neck. ''Okay, Mr. Boswell, what's your suggestion?''

''Well, how about an electrical fault of some kind—a short circuit, causing the gate to close of its own accord?''

The sheriff shrugged. ''Possible. We'll have it checked, of course.'' He looked at Barnes. ''Any signs of that?''

Barnes stared back. ''No,'' he said defiantly, ''and the whole system has regular maintenance checks.''

Millard gave a grunt. ''Okay, you can go. But don't leave the estate.''

Barnes gave a disgusted mutter and ambled off.

''Well, guess I'd better go talk to the family,'' said Millard.

''Mind if I tag along? I'm not the Langley lawyer, but I am an interested party—as the legal representative of the owner of the estate.''

''Reckon I can't stop you, Mr. Boswell, if you want to be there. Come on.''

In the living room they found Morgana and Echo, both in their robes; Spenser, in shirt and slacks; and Jessica and Abby, who were both fully dressed. Abby was sitting on the couch, petting Teddy, who somehow sensed something was wrong.

As the two men entered the room, Morgana turned and came fluttering toward them. Boswell was reminded of a dazed moth making for a candle. She moved close up to Millard and clutched him by the sleeve.

''Sheriff, my brother and daughter say I mustn't tell you this, but I have to. You'll say I'm crazy. But I really saw it!''

The Sheriff drew a sharp breath. ''You saw the accident?''

Morgana shook her head impatiently. "No! I saw my dear sister's ghost rising up from her earthly form and crying like a mourning dove."

"My mother's a little upset, Sheriff," Echo said dryly from across the room.

Morgana swung around to her. "Of course I'm upset! Wouldn't you be if you'd just seen Trish's spirit take wing?"

Millard narrowed his eyes. "Just what you saying, Mrs. Cramer?"

She turned back. "I was looking out of my window—"

"At one o'clock in the morning? May I ask why?"

"I had woken suddenly. I don't know why, but no doubt the sudden destruction of my sister's earthly vessel had set up psychic vibrations that had acted adversely on my—"

"Never mind all that. Tell me what you saw."

"I got out of bed. I often do if I wake at night. My aura thrives on moonlight. It seems actually to feed—" Morgana saw Millard's expression changing and broke off before going on: "Well, I went to the window and looked out. My bedroom is the only one with a view of the main gate through the trees. I saw this figure lying lifeless on the drive. And then, before my eyes, she rose and—and—disappeared." Then, plainly feeling this was an insufficiently mystical expression, Morgana amended it to: "Was absorbed into the ether." She took a deep breath before going on hurriedly. "I ran to tell Spenser. I knocked on his door, but he didn't answer."

"I'm a heavy sleeper," Spenser said irritably. "You know that."

"Tell me, Mrs. Cramer: was the gate open at the time?"

Morgana looked a little taken aback. "Er, yes. That is, I think it must have been."

"Well, your sister was killed by the gate closing, ma'am. It stayed closed till I arrived. If it was open, Miss Langley was still alive. You must have been mistaken."

Morgana gave a helpless little flap of her hands. "It's

not fair,'' she said tearfully. ''My first real ghost, and no one will believe me.''

Millard cleared his throat and addressed the room at large. ''There's some questions I've got to ask.''

But at that moment he was interrupted. A young deputy hurried into the room and whispered excitedly into his ear.

Millard's face suddenly changed to an almost ludicrous extent. His jaw literally dropped. He gazed at the deputy in disbelief, then said hoarsely, ''They—they sure?''

''Absolutely, Sheriff.''

Millard stood, staring blankly in front of him, as though trying to grasp some concept too abstruse for human comprehension. Seconds passed before Spenser asked tersely, ''Sheriff, what's happened? We have a right to know.''

''What? Oh.'' Millard gave a little shake of his head. Then he said, ''Well, folks, seems we got our killer.''

There was an instant hush in the room. Everyone stared at him with bated breath.

''That button in the security room that closes the front gate *was* pressed deliberately. Our boys have found a print on it.''

''A fingerprint?'' Boswell asked.

''Nope. Near as we can figure, it's a paw print.''

It was Spenser who reacted first. ''Teddy? *Teddy* murdered my sister?''

''He pressed the button,'' Millard said.

''That damned dog!'' Spenser hissed the words. ''First he attacks me, then Potts, now he kills Trish.''

''He's evil,'' Morgana whispered. ''He's possessed.'' She backed across to one corner of the room, her eyes fixed with a horrified expression on the dog.

Teddy, once more realizing that he was the center of attention, uttered a little *woof* and wagged his tail.

Morgana gave a muffled scream and began to mutter rapidly under her breath in a strange language. It was, Jessica guessed, some sort of incantation.

Meanwhile, Spenser had turned on Boswell. ''Marcus, that cursed animal has got to go!''

"Oh, and wouldn't *that* be convenient, Spenser," Boswell said sarcastically.

"This is utterly absurd!"

The voice, shaking with emotion, was Abby's. She was on her feet, Teddy in her arms. "Sheriff, you cannot possibly believe a *dog* is capable of murder!"

"Of course he can't," Boswell snapped. "Sheriff, it was obviously just a tragic mischance. Teddy happened to step on the button."

"That won't wash, Mr. Boswell. You've seen the inside of the security room. That hound-dog must've jumped up on Barnes' chair and pressed his paw on the one button out of all of them that'd close the front gate—just at the crucial moment Miss Langley was lying there. Couldn't've been accidental."

"You don't seriously mean to tell me that you believe a dog could work all that out for himself?" Boswell's voice was incredulous.

Millard shrugged. "He did it."

Abby spoke again, her tone one of despair. "But he'd have to be trained. . . ."

The next second she froze, her mouth still open, suddenly realizing the import of her words. Every eye in the room was on her. Teddy turned his head up and tried to lick her chin. She gulped. "Well, I mean—"

"I think we know quite well what you mean, Miss Freestone," Spenser said. He turned to the sheriff. "That woman has hated my sisters and me ever since she came here. She's practically accused us of murdering Father. She verbally attacked Trish on several occasions. She's been in charge of Teddy—and she's a professional animal trainer. If you don't arrest her, you're an even bigger fool than I thought you were until now."

These last words were a mistake. Millard flushed angrily.

Jessica took the opportunity to speak for the first time. "Mr. Langley, are you really implying that Teddy could be trained to recognize your sister on a small black-and-white television screen; realize, when she tripped, that she was in the path of the gate; and seize his opportunity to leap up on the chair and press the button?''

Spenser looked a little taken aback. "Well, no, of course not. I mean—''

"Well said, Mrs. Fletcher," Boswell broke in.

"The sheriff realizes perfectly well," Jessica went on, "that Teddy could only be trained to respond to a direct order—to press the button when he was told to. Anybody can speak to the security room through one of the intercoms scattered around the estate, and that's how the command must have been given. Am I right, Mr. Millard?''

"Yeah." Millard nodded vigorously. "Yeah, that's the way I figured it out.''

"And I'm sure your next question of Mr. Langley was going to be: does he believe my cousin stayed up in the grounds until one A.M., on the off chance that his sister returned home late and just happened to fall and lie unconscious in the path of the gate—and we have Barnes' testimony that that's what happened—so giving Abby the chance to relay the order to Teddy?''

The sheriff looked at Spenser. "Well, what about it, Mr. Langley?''

Spenser shrugged. "According to your own scenario, Mrs. Fletcher, *somebody* did just that—even if it wasn't Miss Freestone. What's your explanation?''

"I don't have one," Jessica said frankly. "I agree, it seems wildly unlikely. But it's certainly *less* unlikely that it should be done by somebody who was conversant with Miss Langley's plans for earlier tonight, and who knew roughly what time to expect her home. I'm quite certain Abby wasn't such a person. I imagine even Mr. Langley would concede that his sister wouldn't have confided in *her*.''

Millard chewed the end of his pencil. He was clearly quite out of his depth. Spenser turned away with a gesture of hopelessness. Abby gave Jessica a mute little nod of thanks.

Jessica looked at her watch. "It's nearly two o'clock,''

she said, "and if you don't require me any longer, Sheriff, I think I shall leave."

He nodded. "That's okay."

"Thank you." She looked at Spenser, Morgana and Echo in turn. "My deepest sympathy in your loss."

Spenser muttered, "Thanks."

Jessica moved to the door. "Coming, Abby?"

Abby stood up. "Is that all right, Mr. Millard? Or am I under arrest?"

"No, no, you can go. But don't leave the estate."

"You've got to be joking," Abby said. She followed Jessica to the door and they went out, Teddy close behind them.

In the hall, Abby drew a deep breath. "Whew, let's get out of here."

"In a moment. Abby, which is Morgana's room?"

Abby raised her eyebrows. "Why on earth—?"

"I'll explain later. Quickly."

"I'm not sure. Let me think." She screwed up her eyes. "I think you turn left at the top of the stairs and it's at the far end of the corridor."

"Right. You go on home. I'll join you shortly."

Jessica hurried up the stairs. Abby looked at her uneasily for a moment, then left the house by the front door, Teddy at her heels.

A few minutes later Jessica arrived back at the top of the stairs and peered cautiously down into the hall. It was clear. Good. It would be highly embarrassing having to explain to the family why she'd been roaming about the upper floors of the house—even though it was for a quite innocent purpose.

She started down the stairs, then stopped as the front door opened. The deputy, Will Roxie, entered. He was carrying a partly folded full-length mink coat and a plastic bag. As she watched, he started trying to roll the coat into a compact bundle and stuff it into the bag. However, it soon became clear the coat was too bulky to go in easily.

Jessica remained motionless for about ten seconds. Then

she continued down the stairs. After all, Will Roxie didn't know she wasn't free to wander all over the house whenever she pleased. As she neared the bottom she said brightly, "Here, Will, let me help you with that."

He looked up. "Oh, hi, Mrs. Fletcher. Thanks. I think this could use a lady's touch. It's just a mite too big for the evidence bag. Thought if I came indoors in the light I'd manage better, but it hasn't really helped."

"I think we'd better start from scratch."

She took the coat from him and shook it out. Will gave a whistle of admiration at seeing it full-length in good light. "Say, my wife sure would give her eyeteeth for this."

"It was taken off the body?"

"Yes, ma'am."

She was staring at the inside of the coat. "Could it have been torn when they were getting it off?"

"Oh no, Mrs. Fletcher. I helped. We were most careful."

"Well, it *is* torn. Look."

She turned the coat inside out for him to see. "This coat's nearly new, I'd say, but the seams are split like my old car coat. Yet I can't imagine Trish Langley wearing it like that for long, can you?"

He frowned. "Meaning it was torn tonight?"

"Well, certainly very recently. Make a note of those splits, Will. They could be important."

"Yes, ma'am. Will do."

He spoke politely, but she fancied he was humoring her. She smiled, helped him fold the coat into a neat and tight bundle and insert it in the bag, said good night, went out and made her way to the cottage.

She found Abby in the kitchen, making a pot of tea.

"As I expected," Jessica said. "Under stress the English always head for the teapot."

"Want a cup?"

"Please."

Abby poured two cups and they went into the living room and sat down.

"Now, why the search of Morgana's room?" Abby asked.

"Oh, not a search. I just wanted to find out exactly what she could see out of her window at night."

"But why? You surely don't believe that crazy story?"

"Well, Morgana's certainly got some weird beliefs, but has there ever been any indication she actually suffers from hallucinations?"

"Not that I know of."

"And I can't think of any reason why she should lie about such a thing."

"You mean you *do* believe her?" Abby's voice was incredulous.

"Not that she saw Trish's spirit leaving her body; of course not. I wanted to find out if she could have seen *anything*—while there were still headlights shining down by the gate and people moving around."

"And could she?"

"Just very small figures. They all look the same height, and naturally you can't see anything of the faces at all. But you can just make out roughly what they're doing."

Abby looked at her curiously. "What are you getting at, Jess?"

"I don't know. I just like to have as many facts as possible." She took a sip of tea. "Abby, how would you go about training Teddy to press that button?"

"Jess! I hope you're not suggesting—"

"Of course not. I'll change the question: how would *one* go about training *a dog* to press it?"

"A simple voice command would suffice. Something like: *Teddy—push*! You'd repeat it over and over, lifting his paw onto the button, until he got it, rewarding him when he did."

Jessica shook her head. "I think it would be too risky to use one's voice. Someone might turn on the intercom and recognize it."

Abby shrugged. "Any sort of sound would do, so long as the dog learned to associate it with the action and respond. A snap of the fingers or a whistle."

"A whistle," Jessica nodded. "That's more like it. Would it take long?"

"Not with a bright young dog like Teddy. He picks things up very quickly."

At that moment there came a knock on the front door. They glanced at each other, then Abby stood up and called, "Who is it?"

"Marcus Boswell."

Abby gave a sigh of relief, crossed and opened it. Boswell came in.

"Thank goodness it's you," said Abby. "I had a horrible feeling that was the sheriff come to arrest Teddy. I was surprised he let me walk out with him."

"Millard doesn't know what he's doing tonight. You were out of the room with the dog before he really noticed. Where *is* Teddy, by the way?"

"Locked in my bedroom. I wasn't taking any chances."

"Good. Though I think we can expect Millard to take Teddy in tomorrow. He'll probably call it protective custody."

Boswell's glance fell on Abby's nearly full teacup on the table.

"Would you like a cup of tea?" Abby asked. "Or something stronger?"

"Tea will be fine. I'd love a cup."

Abby crossed to the kitchen. "Please have a seat," she said.

"Thanks." He lowered himself into an easy chair, stretching his legs out toward the fire.

Jessica noticed that the inside of his right trouser leg, near the bottom, was badly marked with dark stains. She pointed it out to him.

He looked down and gave a grimace. "Oh, great! I had a flat on the way over. Must have got some grease off the jack. I was working more or less in the dark."

Jessica's expression was pensive. "Something wrong?" he asked.

"What? Oh no. Er, whcre was this?"

"Where I had the flat? About half a mile away."

Abby came in with Boswell's tea. She too noticed the expression on Jessica's face. "What's the matter, Jess?"

Jessica smiled. "Probably nothing. But tell me, Mr. Boswell, do you have many flats?"

"No, very few. Why?"

"It's just that I don't like anything even slightly unusual happening in the vicinity of a murder. It just occurred to me to wonder whether your puncture may have been, er, induced."

They both stared at her. Boswell said, "I don't get it."

"Oh, no doubt it's just a coincidence. But suppose the killer wanted to make sure nobody passed the main gate at the time of the murder. I mean, if a car came along at the crucial moment and the driver saw the gate closing on Trish, he might have had time to stop and pull her clear. Some tacks, say, sprinkled across the road half a mile away might have ensured no car *did* come along. Of course, by the time you arrived, the murder had been done, but I don't suppose the killer would have bothered to go back and sweep them up in the interim."

Boswell nodded slowly. "Well, it's a possibility. I must admit it hadn't occurred to me."

"As I say, there's probably nothing to it, but perhaps you could humor me and show me tomorrow just where it happened?"

"Of course, be glad to."

Abby asked, "But, Jess, what will it prove if you do find some tacks?"

"Not a lot. Except that it would be proof positive we're dealing with a highly ingenious and farsighted murderer who carefully planned this murder in advance, down to the smallest detail. It would tell us a lot about his—or her—character; and the better you know your adversary the better your chance of catching him."

Abby smiled to herself. She like that word *adversary* coming from Jessica. At last, it seemed, her cousin was well and truly involved in the Langley affair.

167

Chapter Twenty-one

"AS far as I can remember," Marcus Boswell said, "it was just about here." He pulled into the side of the narrow country road.

"Excuse me," Jessica said, "but if you did go over a tack or something similar, you wouldn't have stopped the same second, would you? I imagine you'd have been going pretty fast. It would have taken fifty or a hundred yards before you realized what had happened and pulled up."

"Yes, you're probably right." Boswell drove on another hundred yards and again stopped. They both got out.

"Suppose we take different sides of the road?" Jessica suggested.

"As you like."

He crossed to the other side, and they began slowly making their way along the highway, heads bent, peering down at the surface. A minute or so passed, and then Boswell jerked his head up sharply at a triumphant cry from Jessica: "Eureka!"

She was kneeling down, her fingers scrabbling at the ground. He hurried across to her. She stood up and proudly held out her hand to him. Lying in the palm were three inch-long, large-headed shiny new tacks.

"Good grief!" Boswell took one of them, an expression of complete amazement on his face.

"You didn't think much of my idea, did you, Mr. Boswell?"

He took a deep breath. "Actually, Mrs. Fletcher, no."

She smiled. "Frankly, Mr. Boswell, on reflection, neither did I. However . . ."

"However, you were right. Congratulations. Are there just the three, I wonder?"

"There seem to be. No doubt the killer *did* come back after and cleared the others away."

"Well, there's no chance of his having left any tire tracks on this road surface."

"In fact," she said regretfully, "it really gets us no farther forward. I'm sure these tacks can be bought in any hardware store, and even if it was possible to find a suspect who'd bought some recently, it would be absolutely no proof he's the murderer. Even if we showed these to the sheriff, I'd be very surprised if he bothered to follow it up."

"I'm afraid you're right. However, it must be very satisfying to have your theory vindicated."

"I do feel quite pleased."

During the latter part of the conversation they'd been retracing their steps to the car. Now Jessica suddenly got down on her hands and knees and stared up at the two front tires. Then she rose, went round to the rear and repeated the procedure.

Boswell looked amused. "A guess: you're wondering if any of my other tires picked up a tack."

"I was, yes. But there's no sign of anything. All the tires look exactly the same. Of course, I couldn't see every section."

"Don't worry, I'll get the garage to check them over."

"Perhaps we could take a look at the wheel you removed last night and see if there's a tack embedded in the tire?"

"Sorry, it's in my garage back home, waiting to be taken in for repair. The one in the trunk now is a second spare I usually keep in the garage. I'll take a look at the other when I get home."

"Good. I'd be interested to know."

"I'll keep you informed. Now, Mrs. Fletcher, I'd better take you back to your cousin's."

*   *   *

When Boswell and Jessica drove up to Abby's cottage, the familiar sight of Sheriff Millard's car met them.

"Uh-uh, I expected this," Boswell said.

They got out and went inside the cottage. They found a tearful Abby confronting a belligerent Millard, while an embarrassed-looking Will Roxie stood by.

"Look, Miss Freestone," Millard was saying, "either you go upstairs and bring that dog down, or we go up and break down your bedroom door. Now which is it to be?"

"What's going on?" Boswell asked coldly.

"They want to take Teddy," Abby explained. "I told them I wasn't letting him go till you got back."

"Mr. Boswell," Millard said, "I've gotta have that dog. I don't know whether he's a suspect or a material witness or an accessory or a clue or an exhibit, but he's sure one of them. He's gotta be kept in protective custody till we clear this business up."

"That means for the rest of his life," Abby snapped.

"I don't think it's any good fighting it, Abby," Boswell told her. "It's probably for the best. We know Teddy will be safe there. And I'm sure we can arrange visiting rights. Better go and get him."

"Very well, if you say so." Abby left the room.

Jessica went after her. They climbed the stairs; Abby took a key from her pocket and opened her bedroom door. Teddy came bounding excitedly out. Abby picked him up and petted him. "Poor old boy. Having to go to prison, just because he does what he's been taught to do."

Jessica spoke on the spur of the moment. "Abby, it won't be for long. I promise you."

Abby stared at her and her eyes widened. "Jess," she said incredulously, "you've solved the case, haven't you?"

"I'm not sure. I'm pretty certain I know how Trish's murder was arranged, but—"

Abby gave a squeal. "Oh Jess, you're wonderful! I knew you'd do it!"

And with Teddy in her arms, she turned and hurried

down the stairs. At the bottom she rushed into the living room and Jessica heard her voice raised elatedly.

"It's all right! You can stop worrying. My cousin's solved the case."

Jessica closed her eyes. Under her breath she murmured, "Oh, no." Hastily she descended the stairs herself. When she entered the living room, every eye was on her. She smiled weakly.

Abby regarded her with pride. "Tell them, Jessica."

"Really, Abby!" Jessica spoke with vexation. "I'm not ready yet."

"Jess, you must talk now, or you'll get bumped off yourself. You know that's what always happens to people who keep silent."

"Yes, do please spill everything, Mrs. Fletcher," Millard said sarcastically. "I'm all ears. This should be a real lesson in police work."

Jessica sighed. "I just have a theory, that's all."

"Better and better. Theories are so much more exciting than boring old facts."

"Sheriff," Boswell snapped, "if you want to hear what Mrs. Fletcher has to say, why don't you just shut up and let her talk? Go on, Mrs. Fletcher."

Jessica took a deep breath. "The problem until now, it seems to me, has been this: even if the killer got Trish drunk, how could he—I'll say *he* for brevity—how could he possibly ensure that she fell right across the path of the gate? Yet the business of training Teddy to press the button proves that that *was* his plan. My idea solves that problem, and explains two other pieces of evidence: what Morgana saw from her window and the fact that the seams of Trish's mink coat were split."

Millard groaned. "Mrs. Fletcher, Morgana's a weirdo. She saw nothing that anyone else would have seen. Trish's coat could have gotten torn anytime."

"Maybe you're right. But I don't think so. Let's look at Barnes' testimony. He saw Trish's car pull up outside the gate at one A.M. Somebody dressed in a fur coat and head scarf got out and pressed the intercom buzzer. Barnes opened the gate, the person fell and Barnes went down to help. Then Morgana looked out of her window and saw the person who'd fallen rise up and, as she put it, disappear. Actually, the person merely moved into the darkness behind the car."

"But she didn't, Mrs. Fletcher!" Millard spoke with exasperation. "Unless Barnes is lying, Trish was still flat on the driveway when he got in sight of the gate."

"What I'm questioning, Mr. Millard, is the word *still*. I don't believe that when Barnes was on his way down from the security room she *was* lying there. I think she'd only been there a matter of seconds when he arrived on the scene."

"Bull! He saw her fall minutes before on his TV screen."

Jessica shook her head. "He saw *somebody* fall. But was it Trish? I think not."

There was a pause. Then Will Roxie suddenly snapped his fingers. "He saw the killer! Dressed in Miss Langley's fur coat."

Jessica beamed at him. "Exactly, Will. Coat and scarf, I think."

Will concentrated. "Miss Langley was very slim and slight, and when the killer put the coat on, it was too small and the seams got split."

"Right."

"But where was Miss Langley then?"

"Lying unconscious —knocked out or drunk or drugged— in the back of the car. I think it was the killer, dressed in Trish's coat and scarf, who drove the car up to the gate. He deliberately slewed it sideways, to suggest drunk driving, got out and staggered to the intercom. But he didn't speak into it—just pressed the buzzer. Barnes could only see a figure outlined against the headlights. He assumed it was Trish and opened the gate.

"The murderer then deliberately fell across the path of the gate, knowing that Barnes would see and come down to help. He gave him a minute to get clear of the security room, then got up, hurried to the back of the car, lifted Trish out, put her things back on her, carried her to the gate and laid her down in the same position he'd been lying himself. Then he used the intercom to give Teddy the command to close the gate. The whole thing must have taken him rather longer than he'd anticipated, because Barnes nearly got there in time to pull Trish clear. However, in the end the plan did work.''

There was silence for several seconds before Will Roxie said softly, ''Gee, that's brilliant.''

Millard shot him a dirty look.

Boswell spread his hands. ''Mrs. Fletcher, for once I'm speechless.''

''What about it, Sheriff?'' Abby asked pointedly.

Millard had taken out his pencil and was engaged in his favorite hobby of chewing the end. At last he gave a reluctant shrug. ''Well, I suppose it makes sense, in a screwy kinda way. But tell me, Mrs. Fletcher, what sort of signal d'you figure he'd give the dog?''

''I don't think he'd use his voice, for fear of it being overheard and recognized. I suggest possibly a whistle.''

Millard reached into his pocket and pulled out a short silver chain from the end of which dangled a shiny whistle. ''Something like this?''

''Yes, I imagine so.''

He put the whistle in his mouth and blew. None of the people in the room heard anything, but Teddy pricked up his ears and gave a bark.

''It's one of them ultrasonic jobs,'' Millard said. ''Only dogs can hear them. We found it in the grass at the edge of the road, about ten yards outside the gate.''

''Well, there you are,'' Jessica said excitedly. ''That's it, for sure.''

''Glad to hear you say that, Mrs. Fletcher, because it's got some initials on it.''

He looked down and read out slowly: ''A.B.F.'' He stared straight at Abby. ''Your middle name's Benton, isn't it, Miss Freestone?''

''Yes.'' Abby had gone very pale.

''That's all I wanted to know. I'm taking you in. Suspicion of murder in the first degree. Read her her rights, Will.''

Looking unhappy, Will took a card from his pocket and approached Abby.

Millard turned to Jessica. "Thanks for fingering her for us, Mrs. Fletcher.''

Jessica gave an indignant gasp. "I did no such thing! Sheriff, this is ridiculous! The fact the killer used Abby's whistle doesn't make Abby the killer.''

"In my book it goes a long way toward it, Mrs. Fletcher.''

Boswell said, "But what conceivable motive could Abby have for murdering Trish?''

Millard shrugged. "There's been bad blood between them. Everybody knows that. Besides, you can never tell—''

"What sort of motives are going to come to light till you start digging—I know, I know.'' Boswell spoke irritably. "Sheriff, Trish might have had a motive for killing Abby, after the accusations Abby's been making about Denton's death. But not the other way around!''

"And what *about* Denton's death?'' Jessica put in. "Isn't it rather a coincidence that there have been two violent deaths in the Langley family in so short a time?''

"Not really. Not if they were both murder.''

Jessica gasped. "But you've refused all along to believe Denton was murdered!''

"There was no real evidence of murder. Trish's death changes things. We now know there's been a killer at large.''

"You're . . . you're not suggesting my cousin murdered *Denton* too?'' Jessica said incredulously.

"Why not? She had a good motive. That horse, Silver King, must be worth thousands of dollars.''

"But, Sheriff,'' Boswell said wearily, "Abby didn't know Denton had left her the horse.''

"Can you be sure of that, Mr. Boswell?''

Boswell looked at Abby. "Tell him, will you?''

Before she could answer, Millard interrupted. "Never mind what she says. Could you, Mr. Boswell, swear Denton Langley didn't tell her?''

Boswell hesitated. "Well, I suppose I couldn't actually—"

"There you are, then. And remember, if Sawdust was doped, this young woman had the best chance of anyone to do it."

Jessica stared at him in disbelief. "But it's Abby who's been insisting, against you and the Langleys, that that's what happened. If she'd done it herself, it would be insane to draw attention to it!"

Millard shrugged again. "Could be a sophisticated double bluff."

Jessica threw her hands in the air. "If you believe that, you'll believe anything."

"Fact is, Mrs. Fletcher, you're kin. You don't want to believe she's guilty. Now, I'm not saying Miss Freestone will be charged with Denton Langley's murder—that'll be up to the DA. But we got enough on her to nail her for Trish's death. And well you know it."

He turned to Abby. "Get your coat, Miss Freestone."

Jessica made one last attempt. "Sheriff, please, give me—"

But she was interrupted. For the last several minutes Abby had been silent. She had merely stood, fondling Teddy, seeming to be only half listening as Jessica and Boswell sought to defend her. There appeared to be a slight smile on her lips. Now, however, she spoke.

"It's all right, Jess. I don't mind. I'm sure you and Mr. Boswell will look after my interests very well. And it means Teddy's going to have a friend with him in the slammer, doesn't it? We can keep each other company."

Chapter Twenty-two

"**W**HY, Mrs. Fletcher, this is a surprise. Do come in."

Tom Cassidy stepped aside, and Jessica entered the house.

"Thank you."

"Go into the den."

He ushered her through a door on the right. She found herself in what was very much the room of an unmarried outdoor man. Sporting trophies lined the walls; stuffed fish were mounted in glass cases; photographs of horses and dogs and groups of men with rifles and fishing rods were dotted about. There was a big open fireplace of undressed stone; deep, shabby but comfortable-looking leather armchairs; bearskin rugs on the floor. There were no flowers or ornaments or anything of purely decorative value.

"Won't you sit down?" Cassidy asked.

Jessica lowered herself into one of the armchairs, sinking so deeply into it that she began to think she would never stop descending.

Cassidy was looking at her as if he didn't quite know what to do with her.

"Can I get you a drink?" he asked abruptly.

"No, really. Thank you."

"Coffee? Tea?"

"Nothing at all, thanks."

"Oh." He fidgeted a little from foot to foot.

"Mr. Cassidy," Jessica said gently, "do forgive me

saying this in your own home, but won't you please sit down?''

"Oh, sure." He took a seat opposite her. He cleared his throat. "I heard about Abby. Very sorry."

"She didn't do it, you know."

"Never thought she did. Millard's a fool."

"You know most people in this neighborhood pretty well, I imagine," Jessica said.

"Sure do. Lived here all my life."

"They look up to you, I'm sure."

He looked embarrassed. "Don't know about that. It was Denton who carried the weight around here."

"But Denton's dead."

"What you getting at, Mrs. Fletcher?"

She paused before asking. "First of all, how well do you know Deputy Roxie?"

"Will? His pa worked for me for thirty years. Will could have, too, if he hadn't decided he wanted a bit more excitement in his life. He's a good boy."

"And rather more intelligent than Sheriff Millard."

"You can say that again. But I don't follow—"

"Well, you see, I'm pretty sure I know who killed Denton and Trish Langley."

He sat up with a jerk. *"You do?"*

"Yes. But unfortunately I have absolutely no proof. I need some help—from someone in a position to make a few inquiries, ask a few questions, take a look at some of the evidence in this case. From somebody in the Sheriff's Department. It's hopeless to ask Millard. Will Roxie seems the obvious man to approach. But I'm an outsider here. Furthermore, I'm Abby's cousin. I think he might be loath to act unofficially, at my request. However, if *you* were to ask him . . ." She left the sentence unfinished.

"Well, of course, I'll do all I can. And I think probably I can persuade Will to do me a favor. I gave him a character reference when he first applied to join the department, so he owes me."

"Oh, that's wonderful."

"What do you want him to do?"

"I'll come to that in a moment. But next let me ask how well you know the coroner?"

"Charlie Harrington? One of my oldest buddies. We've played poker together 'most every Sunday night for the last twenty years."

"Better and better. And he's not, er, hidebound?"

"Not at all. Why?"

"Well, I may want to take part in Trish Langley's inquest. As *amicus curiae*."

"Friend of the court, if I remember my Latin. Rather unusual, isn't it?"

"Yes, but not unheard of. A coroner is allowed a lot of latitude in the way he conducts an inquest. So I'm wondering if you could sound him out on the possibility."

"Yes, of course, if you think it's important."

"I believe it's very important, if we're going to nail the killer."

"Then I think I can guarantee Charlie will play ball." Tom Cassidy chuckled. "I know about one or two things he did in his younger days that he wouldn't want shouted around the town now . . ."

"Oh, I'm not asking you to go in for blackmail."

"There'll be no specific threats, Mrs. Fletcher. But Charlie'll understand. I'm quite adept at arm-twisting when it's really necessary."

Jessica smiled. "I'm not unskilled at it myself. Now, there are a couple more things I want to ask. You've known the Langley children all their lives, I take it."

"Of course."

"Would you give me your impressions of Spenser?"

Cassidy's face clouded slightly. He didn't answer. He reached for a pipe that was resting on a table near his elbow, then withdrew it.

"Please do smoke," Jessica said.

"Oh, thanks."

He filled the pipe from his pouch, lit it and sucked fiercely to get it well glowing. It was a slow, leisurely process, but Jessica did not attempt to hurry it. She knew

Tom Cassidy needed the time to straighten out his thoughts. At last he spoke.

"Must say I've never taken to him."

"May I ask why?"

"Something shifty about him."

"He's a bit of a crook?"

"Well, he doesn't have a criminal record. I don't know anything specific. But I've heard things. And I know Denton was very unhappy about some of Spenser's business deals." He hesitated. "Look, I'm probably being unfair. These are rumors only. I *know* of nothing personally against him."

"I didn't expect you to. I only asked you for your impressions. Has he ever been violent?"

Cassidy glanced at her sharply. "Not that I've ever heard—or seen. Frankly, I doubt he'd have the guts."

"You mean he'd be afraid it would come back on him?"

"Right."

"I see." Jessica was thoughtful for a moment. Then she looked up and spoke more briskly. "Now: what about Morgana?"

Again, Cassidy let several seconds pass before speaking. "Meeting her now, you'd think she was just batty, wouldn't you? But she wasn't always like that. In fact, she was a highly intelligent young woman. She was always interested in the paranormal. But in those days the interest seemed more scientific. She retained some skepticism. Then, after her marriage broke up, she gradually changed. It was as if she began to swallow all that stuff—hook, line and sinker. She seemed to become . . . oh, I don't know, almost a caricature of an occult buff. D'you know what I mean?"

Jessica nodded. "Very well. From the first it seemed to me to be overdone. Spiritualism, astrology, divination, portents—it was just too much."

"That's it. Must admit I found myself wondering once or twice whether it was all genuine. Though for the life of

179

me I can't figure out what reason she could have for pretending."

"Well, you know, in certain circumstances it might suit an intelligent person to be regarded as a bit crazy; not to be taken too seriously; to stand around smiling vaguely, gabbling on about astral projections and auras and spirit guides; and all the time to be listening—picking up all sorts of information other people imagine is going straight over your head. I can conceive of someone getting a kick out of that—secretly laughing all the time at others' gullibility."

He gazed at her in admiration. "Yes, I guess that makes sense. I hadn't seen it that way. You know, Mrs. Fletcher, I understand why you're a successful author."

"Because I have such a vivid imagination?"

"Not really. Because you understand how other people's minds work—you can put yourself in their shoes."

Jessica smiled. "It's not always a fortunate ability. Sometimes I try to put myself in the shoes of a murderer, and, really, I often begin to feel quite murderous. But to revert, what do you know about Echo?"

"Not a lot. Haven't seen much of her. She hasn't been here a great deal. What I've seen I rather like. She's a cheeky young minx, but she's got spirit. I feel a little sorry for her, though. . . . Mrs. Fletcher, you say you think you know who killed Denton and Trish. So may I ask just what's the point of these questions?"

"You're wondering if it's just pure nosiness? Well, no. I admit that not everything I've asked is relevant to the identity of the murderer. But I want to tie up all the loose ends before I make my presentation in court, and an independent opinion on the character of some of the people involved should be a help. I promise you that everything you've said will remain quite confidential. I may be inquisitive. But I'm not a gossip."

"I never thought you were, ma'am."

Jessica opened her purse and took from it a folded piece of paper. "Now, these are the points I'd like you to have Will check out for me."

Cassidy took it and read it through slowly. The expres-

sion on his face changed from blankness to mystification
and finally to anger. He looked up.

"If this points the way it seems to—"

"There's no proof as yet," she said. "That's why those
things are so important. Particularly the first. That should
be followed up immediately; otherwise it could be too late.
It's a long shot, but it could provide proof positive."

Cassidy stood up. "I'll get on to it right away. And if
Will can't do it, I'll check it out myself."

Jessica also rose. "Thank you very much. Will you call
me as soon as you find out anything?"

"Sure will."

"Good. And now you can do one more thing for me:
tell me how to get to Asa Potts' place. I have to see a man
about a dog bite."

Asa Potts' farm looked a mess. Paint peeled from the
woodwork, a window was boarded up. The gate into the
yard, which was littered with junk, hung crookedly from
its post. A shed looked on the verge of collapse. A few
scrawny-looking hens pecked listlessly about.

It was a depressing sight, Jessica thought, as she gazed
at it from the shelter of a clump of trees. There was no
sign of human life. However, the next moment there came
the sound of a power saw from the far side of the house.

Jessica glanced around, then left the trees. She made her
way up to the crooked gate and entered the yard. She
crossed it and peered cautiously around the side of the
house.

Asa Potts, in scruffy old jeans and a checked shirt
with the sleeves rolled up, was cutting logs. His back was
to her, and Jessica was able to eye him at leisure for
several seconds. She paid particular attention to his arms.
They told her all she needed to know; and she was about to
turn away when a voice from behind her nearly made her
jump out of her skin.

"Is this just a social call, Mrs. Fletcher?"

She spun around. Spenser Langley was standing about
six feet away. His face was cold and hard.

Jessica rallied. "I might ask you the same question, Mr. Langley."

"Potts is a neighbor of mine. The properties adjoin. Naturally, we have common interests."

Jessica nodded. "Yes, I'm sure you have."

The sound of the saw had stopped and she heard footsteps behind her. She turned again to see Potts staring suspiciously at her. In his hands was a shotgun.

"What you doing here?" he growled.

"I came to see how you were recovering."

"Recovering?"

"From that very bad bite you received from Teddy. I must say your healing process is quite remarkable. There's not a mark of any kind on your arm, not the slightest sign of a scar."

"You fool, Potts," Spenser said viciously.

Potts' complexion went red. "Less of the fool, mister. This was your crazy idea. I should never have listened to you."

Jessica looked at Spenser again. "Did you really expect to get away with drugging Teddy and having this man fake an injury?"

For a moment it seemed Spenser was going to deny the charge. Then he obviously realized the futility of this.

"Having the dog destroyed seemed the surest way to break the will," he muttered.

"Where did the blood on Teddy's collar come from?"

"Potts pricked his finger and we smeared it on."

Jessica nodded. "I see. That was before Boswell put the dog in Abby's full-time care, so you had easy access to him. Then you drugged him to make him attack you. You pretended to stop Potts' showing his wound to the sheriff that day. I suppose you figured that with Potts' blood on the collar, witnesses to testify the dog *had* attacked *you*, plus Potts' artistically bandaged arm, no one would think to question that he had actually been bitten by the dog."

"But *you* did, of course, Mrs. Fletcher," Spenser sneered.

"Oh, I'm sure if the case ever came to trial, Mr. Boswell would demand medical proof of the bite."

Spenser grinned. "That could have been forthcoming—if needed."

"Ah, I see." Jessica nodded comprehendingly. "Yes, Mr. Langley, you would be the sort of person to be acquainted with a certain type of amenable doctor."

Spenser bowed. "I take that as a compliment."

Suddenly Potts' gave a yell. "Shut up this gabble!" He glared at Spenser. "You're playing into her hands—admitting everything. You call *me* a feel!"

"She knows!" Spenser snapped. "Once she'd seen your arm, there was no point in denying it."

Potts stepped menacingly up to Jessica. "We'll go to jail for this unless we shut her up."

"And how do you propose to do that?"

"I been to jail once and I ain't going back." He brandished the shotgun. "I say we plant her in the orchard."

Jessica's heart missed a beat. The man looked and sounded deadly serious. But the next moment Spenser stepped forward. He brushed past her, strode up to Potts and twisted the gun from his hands. "Don't be such a damned hillbilly, Potts," he said curtly. He addressed Jessica. "He's harmless, really. Just likes to talk big."

Potts was looking sulky. "We could have scared her into keeping her trap shut."

"I don't think Mrs. Fletcher is the type to be scared into keeping her trap shut."

He looked back at her again. "Mrs. Fletcher, this was a crazy scheme, born of desperation. We would have needed to prove at least one other attack by Teddy, before he would have been destroyed. But now everything's changed: my sister's dead and Teddy's in the sheriff's charge. The scheme is kaput. Potts won't press the matter any further. So, can't you forget it? After all, what real harm have we done?"

Jessica was silent for a few moments. She glanced from Spenser to the still truculent-looking Potts and back to Spenser before answering. "Well, I don't know what the ASPCA would think of your giving Teddy that drug, but it didn't seem to do him any lasting harm. Nonetheless, it *was* a clear attempt at fraud."

"Guilty. I attempted to defraud a dog out of fifteen million bucks."

In spite of herself, Jessica smiled. She said, "I'll compromise. I shall say nothing about Mr. Potts' part in this." She almost felt Potts relax at these words. She continued, addressing Spenser, "And I'll say nothing about your part in it—providing you make no further attempt to overturn the will. If you do, I shall tell Mr. Boswell all I know."

Spenser pursed his lips. "You drive a hard bargain, ma'am."

"Take it or leave it."

He made a gesture of resignation. "Done."

Jessica took a deep breath. "Very well. And now, if you'll excuse me, I'll be getting along."

"I'll excuse you, all right," Potts grunted. "Didn't ask you here in the first place."

"Forgive my friend," Spenser said smoothly. "I assure you that beneath his rough exterior beats a heart of gold. Allow me to escort you to the gate."

They crossed the yard together and he opened the gate. Jessica went through.

"Thank you," she said. "Goodbye."

As she was walking away he called out after her. "Oh, Mrs. Fletcher."

She turned. "Yes?"

"You understand, my promise is solely personal. Morgana and Echo had no part in my little scheme, and I have no influence over what they decide to do about contesting the will."

He raised a hand in final salute, turned around and sauntered back across the yard. Jessica watched him for a moment, then continued on her way, beset by the sudden vague suspicion that somehow she had been conned.

However, she soon threw off the feeling. Compared with murder, a simple fraud was not very important. It was the murder she had to concentrate on. As long as she cleared Abby, nothing else really mattered.

Chapter Twenty-three

THE courtroom was packed to overflowing. The bizarre circumstances of Trish Langley's death, coming immediately after that of her father, followed by the arrest of Abby, and finally the knowledge of Jessica's involvement, had aroused tremendous media interest. Neither in the press gallery nor on the public benches was there an empty seat. Certainly in all his years as county coroner, Charles Harrington had never known an inquest like it.

The clock showed eleven A.M. He banged with his gavel on the desk, and a hush settled on the courtroom. He made a few preliminary remarks, formally stating the purpose of the proceedings. Official evidence of identification was given, and then the medical examiner was called to stipulate the cause of death. After this a fingerprint expert testified to having visited the security room with Barnes, finding Teddy there alone, locked in, and to his discovery of the dog's paw print on the gate button. He produced the actual button, still set in its mounting, which had been removed from the security room.

When he had stepped down, the coroner said, "This hearing is now going to take rather an unusual turn. I have been informed that a lady who was staying on the Langley estate at the time of the tragedy believes she can, by means of a demonstration, throw light on how it came to occur. Somewhat against my better judgment I have agreed to let her present this demonstration, in the capacity of *amicus curiae*. I've also decided it better be gotten out of the way at the outset, as it may affect the entire course of the hearing. I just hope it isn't going to turn out to be a mare's nest; if so, certain people will have a great deal of explaining to do.''

He glared pointedly at Tom Cassidy, who raised a hand to his mouth to conceal a smile.

''Mrs. Fletcher,'' Harrington said.

Jessica rose and stepped forward. ''Thank you, sir.''

She coughed nervously. ''As you know—as probably everybody knows—Abigail Freestone has been charged with the murder of Trish Langley, the accusation being that she trained the dog, Teddy, to press the button which operated the gate and so killed Trish. Apart from the fact that Abigail Freestone is an experienced animal trainer, the only real evidence against her is that a whistle belonging to her was found by the sheriff's men, lying in the grass near the intercom at the gate where Trish Langley was killed.''

She crossed to a table where the various exhibits, neatly labeled, were laid out, picked up the whistle and held it in the air. ''This is it. Sheriff Millard believes this was used to give Teddy the signal to press the button. I now wish to call my only witness—and that is Teddy.''

She made a sign to Will Roxie, who was standing by the door. He went out and reappeared a moment later, leading Teddy on a leash. In his other hand Will was carrying a small loudspeaker, from which trailed a long electric wire. The other end of it remained outside the courtroom. He placed the loudspeaker on the table, then looked down at the dog and said, ''Sit.''

Teddy sat down and looked around expectantly.

''I think we'll dispense with a swearing-in,'' Harrington said. A titter was heard throughout the room.

Jessica addressed the coroner. ''This loudspeaker has been supplied by the company that installed the security system at Langley Manor. It is identical to the ones used in the intercoms there.''

She handed the whistle to Will. ''Would you blow into this, please?''

Will complied. Teddy's ears instantly pricked, his head jerked up and he gave a bark.

"Of course," Jessica went on, "that is an ultrasonic whistle, audible only to a dog. And there can be no question but that Teddy heard it. Now, Will, I'd like you to go outside into the room on the far side of the corridor. Make sure both doors are closed, speak into the mike that's hooked up to this speaker—and then blow the whistle again."

Will gave a nod and went out. The tension in the room could almost be tasted during the few seconds' silence that ensued before Will's voice came over the intercom.

"I'm ready, ma'am. Going to blow now."

There was a pause. Every eye was fixed on Teddy. But the dog reacted not at all. He was in fact beginning to look rather bored. Then Will spoke again.

"That's it. I gave a long, hard blow."

Jessica turned to the coroner. "You see, sir, even Teddy couldn't hear it this time."

Harrington frowned. "Why not?"

"Because that whistle is above the range of any loud-speaker. The chief electronic engineer of the company is in court and will testify to that effect, if required. The whistle *couldn't* have been the killer's signal. Therefore, the main piece of evidence against Abigail Freestone is quite worthless."

In her seat, Abby was smiling with relief and joy. Boswell gave her a delighted thumbs-up sign. The sheriff's expression was sour, while the faces of Spenser, Morgana and Echo showed no expression at all.

"Well, that's quite remarkable," Harrington said. "You suggesting that whistle was planted in order to incriminate your cousin, Mrs. Fletcher?"

Jessica shrugged. "Obviously it *could* have been. I'm not claiming it *was*. It might have been pure coincidence."

"Hm. Mighty farfetched one. Do you have any idea as to what the signal actually was?"

"I think so. Mr. Barnes—the security guard—and Morgana Cramer have both described something that sounded like a bird call: Mr. Barnes told me it was a mockingbird, Mrs. Cramer described it as 'crying like a mourning dove.' That, I believe, was the signal. This could perhaps be proved by having someone imitate that call and seeing if Teddy reacts.''

The coroner considered. "I think we'll skip that for now."

"I believe it's important," Jessica persisted.

"No, I don't see it, Mrs. Fletcher. We know a signal *was* given—the paw print on the button proves that—and if it wasn't the whistle, the exact nature of it is irrelevant. Moreover, anyone could learn to imitate a mockingbird."

He signaled to the bailiff. "Take the dog out, please."

The bailiff complied, and Harrington addressed Jessica again. "Well, thank you very much, Mrs. Fletcher. You've not, of course, exposed the real murderer, but on the other hand—"

Jessica interrupted. "I think I can, sir."

He stared at her. "You saying you know who killed Trish Langley?"

"I believe the evidence all points in one direction. May I proceed?"

"Yes, Mrs. Fletcher, do. Irregular this may be, and I daresay I'll be criticized, but if there's a chance to clear this business up, I say let's try. You turned up trumps over the whistle, so the floor's yours."

"Thank you, Mr. Coroner." Jessica looked around the court. "I was very much confused immediately after Trish Langley's death, because it seemed obviously linked with other attempts by certain, er, interested parties, to have Teddy destroyed, thereby upsetting Denton Langley's will."

She looked hard at Spenser. He was sweating, but his face remained expressionless. Jessica let him worry for a few more moments, then went on: "Actually, the murder of Trish was unconnected with the attempts on Teddy's reputation—unconnected except insofar as the latter provided a perfect cover for Trish's killer.

"Now, why was Trish Langley killed? Not for money. *Denton* Langley was killed for money. His horse was doped to make it bolt. And the person who doped it was"—Jessica paused—"Trish Langley."

She stopped to let this sink in, then continued: "Trish, however, had an accomplice—someone who probably put her up to doping Sawdust, and who then killed her to prevent her talking and revealing her accomplice's identity, perhaps even blackmailing that accomplice. For, after all, fifteen million dollars was at stake."

"But, Mrs. Fletcher," the coroner said, "Trish only inherited fifty thousand dollars under Denton's will."

"Yes, sir, but she had expected to get millions. Instead, she saw practically all her father's money go to Teddy. One can imagine the shock, and the furious anger when she learned the truth. She was bitter, revengeful and almost constantly drunk. She'd been drinking the night she was murdered. She was a dangerous woman who had to be silenced. The murderer's scheme was highly ingenious, and very complex. Everything had to be timed, almost to the second. Barnes had to be lured from the security room. Nobody had to be near. The road had to be clear. And it was that thought that really led me to the truth."

"You're losing me, Mrs. Fletcher," Harrington said.

"I'm sorry. Perhaps I'm not expressing myself clearly. I'll try to explain." She thought for a moment. "The night of the murder, something rather fortunate happened." She smiled. "Mr. Boswell came to my cousin's cottage, and I happened to notice that he had grease on his trousers. I pointed it out to him, and as a result he told me something he would otherwise never have bothered to mention: he'd had a flat tire on his way over and had had to change a wheel. I immediately suggested that the puncture may have been deliberately caused—that the killer might have strewn tacks or something similar in the road to make sure it remained free of traffic at the time of the murder.

"Mr. Boswell didn't think a lot of the idea, but he agreed to come with me to the spot he'd had his flat, and search for something which may have caused it. After we'd been examining the road surface for a few minutes, I was able to show him three large tacks. Mr. Boswell took one of them, and I'm sure he'd agree it could easily have caused a puncture.''

She glanced at Boswell and he gave a brief nod. Jessica went on.

"Unfortunately, we weren't able to examine the punctured tire there and then, as Mr. Boswell explained it was at home in his garage, waiting to be taken in for repair.''

Jessica gave a signal to Will Roxie, who had reentered the courtroom several minutes earlier. He came forward, producing from his pocket a small pillbox, which he handed to her. She opened it and took from it a small shiny object, which she held up. "And this is, in fact, the very tack that later that day the mechanic at Wilson's garage removed from Mr. Boswell's tire in the presence of Deputy Roxie.''

The coroner was looking keenly interested. He leaned forward. "Mrs. Fletcher, it's evident that whoever put those tacks on the road is the killer. Are you saying you know who that person was?''

"Yes, sir.''

"Do you have proof?''

"Better than that, I think. I have a confession.''

"A confession?'' The coroner stared. "Then for heaven's sake, Mrs. Fletcher, don't keep us in suspense. Tell us who did it.''

Once more Jessica's eyes swept the room. They alighted finally on Tom Cassidy. Then she looked back at the coroner.

"I did,'' she said.

A buzz of mystified excitement ran through the courtroom at Jessica's words. The faces of most of the principals were blank with bafflement, but Marcus Boswell was looking extremely angry.

Charles Harrington silenced the room with a further bang of his gavel. Then he looked sternly at Jessica.

"Is this a joke, Mrs. Fletcher?''

"No, sir.''

"I take it that you are not confessing to the murder of Trish Langley?''

"No, I'm not."

"I think you had better explain." The coroner's voice was edged with ice.

"Certainly." She held up the tack again. "This is one of three tacks, taken by me from the tool closet at the Langley Manor stables. It can be positively identified, because I scratched my initials on the underside of the head. The lettering is naturally very small, but it can be clearly seen with a magnifying glass. I marked it before dropping it on the road at approximately the spot that Mr. Boswell identified as the place where he'd had his puncture."

She paused. "And that, Mr. Coroner, is really very strange. Because, you see, I'd dropped these tacks just a few seconds before pretending to find them there—twelve hours *after* Mr. Boswell's supposed puncture."

There was absolute hush in the courtroom. It was Marcus Boswell himself who eventually broke it. His face was livid as he jumped to his feet.

"Mr. Coroner, I must protest! I—"

"Please sit down, Mr. Boswell. You'll have a chance to speak later. Continue, Mrs. Fletcher."

Jessica collected her thoughts. "The truth," she said, "is that Mr. Boswell did *not* have a flat. He made that up on the spur of the moment, in order to account for the grease marks on his trouser leg. However, when I showed such an interest in his story, he had to carry on with it. Even to the extent of deliberately puncturing one of his tires. When he and I were out together, I looked at the tires on his car. They all showed a virtually identical amount of wear—a pretty clear indication that none of them was the usual spare, and that a wheel had *not* been changed. I asked to see the tire that had received the puncture, but Mr. Boswell claimed it was back in his garage. He obviously couldn't allow me to see the spare wheel—untouched and intact—in the trunk."

Again Boswell was on his feet, shouting. "Mr. Coroner, this is irrelevant, immaterial, and just plain inane!"

The coroner hesitated. "Well, Mrs. Fletcher: is it? You

are certainly attributing strange behavior to Mr. Boswell.
But if a man wants to puncture his own tire, I can't see it's
evidence of any crime."

"Not *evidence*, I agree," Jessica said. "But when someone does all that to cover up his true actions on the night
of a murder, it is surely suspicious. The fact is, as soon as
I saw the grease on Mr. Boswell's trouser leg, I recognized it for what it was: the *mark left by a bicycle chain*.
Mr. Boswell had been riding a bike that night—and he
didn't want anybody to know it."

"And why do you say that was?"

Jessica spoke very deliberately. "Because he used the
bike to get away from the scene of the murder after killing
Trish Langley."

Once more Boswell leapt up. His face was now con-
vulsed with fury. "This is monstrous!" he yelled. "It's
character assassination!"

"It's certainly a very grave accusation," Harrington
said. "Do you have anything to support it, Mrs. Fletcher?
Anything concrete?"

Jessica went back to the table and picked up one of the
exhibits. "This is a bicycle clip. Now, marks such as
those on Mr. Boswell's trousers are only made when clips
are not worn. This clip was found in the long grass by the
sheriff's men during their routine search of the area around
the main gate of the Langley estate."

"But . . . but absolutely anybody could have dropped
that!" Boswell spluttered.

Jessica looked at him. "But you do own a bicycle?"

"Sure I do. So do millions of other people." He turned
to Harrington. "Mr. Coroner, how much longer do we
have to put up with this—this comedy routine?"

"And when," Jessica asked, "is Mr. Boswell going to
explain why he deliberately punctured his own tire?"

Boswell threw up his hands in a gesture of surrender.
"All right. I'll explain. I *did* have to change a wheel that
night. But not on *my* car. I was out with a lady—in her
car. We had a flat. I lied to Mrs. Fletcher about it because

the lady I was with is married. And before anybody asks, I have no intention of revealing her name.''

There was silence. Harrington drummed with his fingers on the desk. He looked from the flushed and breathless Boswell to Jessica.

''Well, Mrs. Fletcher, do you have anything else to substantiate your claim? Because that seems a pretty reasonable explanation to me.''

Jessica nodded. ''It is. I congratulate Mr. Boswell on thinking of it. But, of course, it's completely untrue.''

Boswell opened his mouth for an angry retort, but before he could speak Jessica went on.

''Mr. Coroner, I think this could be settled once and for all. Earlier, I asked to be allowed to conduct a further experiment with Teddy. You refused to allow it. May I respectfully repeat my request? It will only take a matter of a minute or two.''

There was what seemed a very long pause while Harrington considered. Although she was outwardly calm, Jessica's heart was in her mouth. This was her last ace. If the coroner refused to let her play it, or Boswell trumped it, she was finished—and heaven only knew what sort of slander charges she had laid herself open to.

At last Harrington spoke. ''All right, Mrs. Fletcher, I will give you just a little more latitude. But I warn you, this is the end. Prove your case now, or that's it as far as this court is concerned.'' He spoke to the bailiff. ''Bring the dog back.''

Jessica drew a deep breath. Now, if only Teddy cooperated. This was about the longest long shot she had ever played in her life.

She went across to the witness table, picked up the gate button in its mounting and moved it to a position clear of the other exhibits. Next she pulled a chair up to the table, so that it was just a foot or so from the button.

The bailiff had returned, leading Teddy. ''Unclip his leash and lift him on to the chair, please,'' Jessica said.

The bailiff glanced at the coroner, and on receiving a brief nod, complied. Jessica picked up the button, held it out for the dog to sniff and replaced it. Teddy, highly alert, gave a little whine and fixed his eyes on it.

Jessica stepped back and looked at Barnes, seated in the witness benches. "Now, please, Mr. Barnes."

Barnes cleared his throat, pursed his lips, and the next moment a passable imitation of the distinctive call of the mockingbird rang out.

Teddy stood up. He placed his front paws on the table. His head on one side, his ears pricked, he gazed down at it. Then he deliberately lifted his right paw and pressed it firmly onto the button.

A communal sigh, like wind in the trees, was heard in the courtroom as the breath was slowly expelled from a hundred pairs of lungs.

But Teddy had not finished his performance. Suddenly he jumped down from the chair. The bailiff made as if to grab him, but Jessica quickly checked him with a raised hand. Teddy trotted across the courtroom to the spectator benches. He stopped, sat down, then raised his front legs and begged. He gazed up trustingly straight into the face of Marcus Boswell.

Jessica's voice rang out triumphantly. "Why don't you feed him his reward, Mr. Boswell? After all, he learned to expect it when you were training him to help you murder Trish."

For a full ten seconds Marcus Boswell stared mutely down. Then he slowly bent forward and fondled the dog's ears.

"Sorry, boy," he said huskily, "I just don't have any treats on me right now."

He straightened up, leaned back and covered his face with his hands.

Chapter Twenty-four

"JESS, I don't understand," Abby said plaintively.

"Must admit I'm a bit flummoxed, too," Tom Cassidy added.

They both gazed hopefully at her. Even Teddy's limpid eyes seemed to be entreating her for something, though in his case it was no doubt for another piece of chocolate cake.

Jessica smiled. "You want an explanation?"

"Yes, please." Abby and Tom spoke in unison.

"Very well." She settled back in Abby's easy chair. "I suppose the first important thing to grasp, which really nobody did at first, is that in leaving the bulk of his estate to Teddy and appointing Marcus Boswell executor, Denton Langley was in effect leaving the money to his attorney— putting him in virtual control of fifteen million dollars. I'm sure Boswell would have found a hundred clever ways to rake off all he wanted. He must have realized the potential as soon as Denton told him of his intention. The trouble then was that Denton might easily live for another fifteen years, or even longer—and Boswell needed money urgently."

"How do you know that?" Abby asked. "He always seemed very prosperous."

"I suppose I don't *know* it. It may have been just greed that drove him. But do you remember the day you and I visited him, his secretary told him that somebody named Bob Hawkins had tried three times to contact him and that it was vital. I asked you afterwards if you knew who

Hawkins was, and you said you only knew that a man by that name had been Denton's broker. It was, then, quite likely he was Boswell's broker, too. Now, I don't know a lot about the brokerage business, but I don't imagine brokers often ring up just to ask how you're feeling. If a broker calls a client three times in one day, and says it's vital, then it's a pretty safe bet he's not phoning to tell him that his stocks are all doing very nicely. That sort of urgency usually means he wants money—and fast.''

Tom said, ''And so that was one of the things you wanted me to have Will Roxie check out for you.''

''Well, it's very much easier for someone with a badge to ask that sort of question. Anyway, Will later got it confirmed by Mr. Hawkins that Boswell *had* suffered a disastrous loss, through some highly speculative stock he'd bought—against Hawkins' advice. So it was a fair guess he was badly off, in spite of his outward appearance of prosperity.''

''But surely you weren't suspicious of him from that day we called there, were you?'' Abby asked.

''No, I wouldn't say really suspicious. But something else you'd told me earlier had already made me, er, Boswell-conscious, shall we say. You'd mentioned that at the will-reading Trish was furious with him, swore she would never forgive him, was going to get even, and so on.''

Tom Cassidy nodded thoughtfully. ''Yes, I remember. I thought it was odd. Granted, she was bitterly disappointed; but it wasn't Boswell's fault. Denton was his own man. Boswell could never have talked him into making that will. You think she was really mad because Boswell had told her she was going to inherit a lot of money?''

''Well, I'm certain she wouldn't have tried to kill her father for a mere fifty thousand dollars. That would be chicken feed to a girl like her.''

''Can you be sure it was Trish who doped Sawdust?'' Tom asked.

''It's not a mathematical certainty, but I can't see any other explanation that fits all the facts. After all, if Boswell were going to do it himself, he had no need to involve

Trish at all. I think the *method* was Boswell's idea. It has his touch.''

Abby frowned. "How do you mean?"

"He's a gambler. We know that from his stock dealings. This was a gamble. There was a fair chance Denton would be killed, but it was far from certain. Like the murder of Trish herself—so much could have gone wrong with that, from his point of view. I think he got a kick from that uncertainty.''

"I still don't see how, if she doped Sawdust, she could be a threat to Boswell," Tom said. "She couldn't talk about what they'd done. So why did he have to kill her?''

Jessica smiled. "You're looking at it from a very cool, rational, sober—and masculine—point of view. Trish was bitter, revengeful, a woman—and, above all, a drunk. She could have easily worked herself into such a state that she didn't care how much she incriminated herself, just so she got even. No, she clearly had to go.''

"When did you first suspect Boswell of her murder?" Abby asked.

"I think when he lied about the grease on his trousers. You see, I've been cycling all my life, and I knew instantly what that mark was. It's so characteristic. I've stained my own slacks in exactly the same way. So I was staggered when he came out with that story about changing a wheel. Why should he lie? I knew I had to dig deeper. But I didn't want him to realize I was suspicious; I needed a pretext for questioning him more closely about it. So I made up that ridiculous suggestion that the killer had sprinkled tacks on the road to keep it free from traffic.''

Abby stared. "You never really thought that had happened?''

"Not for a moment. But then I decided to make use of the idea. Before Boswell and I went out together the next day, I initialed those three tacks and then pretended to find them on the road. It really shook him. He didn't know what to make of it. It gave me an opportunity to look closely at his tires, to satisfy myself they were all evenly worn, and that therefore a wheel had almost certainly *not* been changed. I asked to see the so-called flat tire—but he had to pretend he'd left it at home.

"Why should he go to such lengths to conceal the fact that he'd been riding a bike? And then it came to me. I'd already worked out how the murder had been done—the killer donning Trish's mink, lying down in the path of the gate, and so on. I realized that he must have had some silent and fairly rapid means of getting away from the scene of the crime. A bike would have been ideal—either carried in the trunk or concealed in the bushes in advance. He could have cycled to wherever he'd parked his car and driven home just in time to take Barnes' phone call.

"It all slotted into place. Teddy knew Boswell, who'd given him to Denton in the first place. Boswell had the opportunity to teach him that business with the gate button. I bet all those so-called walks he took Teddy on were actually spent in the security room."

Abby looked surprised. "Surely Barnes wasn't in on it?"

"Oh no. I expect it was during Smedley's shifts. No doubt he was just told to go off duty and leave Boswell alone there with the dog. I expect Boswell made it well worth his while to keep quiet about it."

Tom raised his eyebrows. "Rather putting himself in Smedley's power, wasn't he?"

Jessica shrugged. "If you decide to commit any crimes, there's the possibility of that risk. In this case the risk wasn't too great. Smedley wouldn't have any concrete evidence against him; he could only threaten to tell the sheriff that Boswell had spent time in the security room with the dog. Boswell could buy his silence for a while, and then I'm sure he could have contrived some equally ingenious way to dispose of Smedley. Or, on the other hand, we don't know that—as an attorney—he didn't have some hold over Smedley to ensure his silence."

"All right," Abby said, "you'd decided Boswell was the murderer and worked out nearly all the details of how he'd done it. What next?"

"I really wanted confirmation and clarification. First of

all, I knew that Boswell, having started on this flat-tire story, would have to go through with it to the end. He couldn't risk the fact that he *hadn't* taken any tire in for repair coming to light. He'd have to give one of his tires a puncture. And, as he'd kept one of my tacks, it was an odds-on bet he'd use that to do it.''

Tom Cassidy nodded. "Which explains the first commission you had me give Will: find out what garage Boswell used and take possession of anything they discovered embedded in his tire."

"Correct. I knew that however well Boswell had covered his tracks, he'd have a tough job explaining the deliberate puncturing of his own tire. Actually, in the event, he fought back brilliantly—though obviously it would have been almost impossible for him to maintain that story about the married woman indefinitely."

Tom said, "You also had me ask Will if they'd found a bicycle clip near the scene of the murder. You even anticipated that!"

"It wasn't vitally important. But cyclists usually keep a pair of clips handy—sometimes in a saddlebag or basket. If Boswell had been cycling without clips, or with only one, it was in the cards he'd dropped one in the dark and hadn't had time to search for it. It was another point confirming my theory. But I couldn't think of any way to prove it. Remember that my primary purpose was to clear Abby. I realized that a demonstration of some kind would be the best way to achieve both ends. The only time and place at which I knew all the necessary persons and things would be brought together—Boswell, Teddy, the exhibits, witnesses—was the inquest."

"And that's when you came to me," Tom said.

"That's right, and you helped no end. You were also able to assist me in clearing up the problem of the remaining Langleys."

"How was that?"

"Well, there was just a possibility one of them was involved in some way. Could one of them have been in cahoots with Boswell—perhaps in helping to overpower

Trish, or carrying her unconscious body? There was no obvious motive, but Boswell *might* have promised one of them a share in the estate for helping to dispose of her. I knew Abby's opinion of the Langleys. But you had known them much longer—since they were children. You largely confirmed her opinion of them. But you added a little. First, you said that Spenser had never been violent and that he lacked the guts to be. But there remained the matter of the attempt to frame Teddy. Somebody had been responsible for that. I went over to Potts' farm, and by a stroke of luck got proof that his claim of being bitten was a lie. I also ran into Spenser, learned that he had been behind the scheme, and that it was true he wasn't of a violent nature. I was convinced then that the doping of Teddy and the murder of Trish were unconnected—and I mentally cleared Spenser of any involvement in his sister's death. There remained the enigmatic figure of Morgana. And there again you helped me. Do you remember what you said about her?''

He thought. "Only that as a girl she was very intelligent.''

"That's it. You see, all along I'd been puzzled by Morgana's statement about what she'd seen from her window. I could think of no conceivable reason she should invent such a story. On the other hand, could even the most dedicated believer in the supernatural really imagine that what she'd seen was a ghost? She'd watched an actual flesh-and-blood person standing up and walking away—not a spirit materializing and leaving the body behind. But after what you said, Tom, I realized Morgana's vagueness and eccentricity might be a façade. It occurred to me that perhaps she had understood fully what she'd seen, and that describing it in those terms had been her means of obliquely giving a clue to the sheriff and yet not getting too involved. That way her statement made much better sense. And it virtually ruled out the possibility of Morgana being involved in the murder.''

"It didn't rule out Echo, though,'' Abby said.

"True. But it meant that if she *was* involved, Morgana didn't have the slightest suspicion of it. She would never've mentioned what she'd seen if she thought she might be incriminating her daughter. Morgana, of course, might not have known if Echo was involved. But I didn't really see Boswell seeking the help of a girl like Echo. It was just a possibility, but a very slight one, and there was nothing much I could do about it, anyway.

"Then, as I had Will Roxie's reports—on Boswell's stock-market losses, the finding of the tack in the tire, and the bicycle clip—I became absolutely certain that he was the killer, and that he'd played a lone hand. I knew he was the one I had to concentrate on."

"But you really concentrated on Millard first, didn't you?" Abby said. "On demolishing his case against *me*."

"That didn't entail a lot of work. I just called on the chief engineer of the security company and learned your whistle couldn't have been used to signal to Teddy over the loudspeaker, borrowed some of their equipment, and got the engineer's promise to testify at the inquest, if necessary. I wasn't worried about that part of the demonstration. I knew it had to work. But the second one involving Teddy—that was a different matter. I didn't even know Teddy would react to the button in the same way in such a different environment. And then, the mockingbird's call was going to be slightly different from the original—though I had spoken to Barnes and asked him to practice imitating the call he had heard as closely as possible, and be prepared to reproduce it at the inquest. But even if Teddy did press the button in the courtroom, that would really prove nothing. It was what he did after that which was vitally important. I don't think I've ever been so nervous in my life as in those few seconds."

"What gave you the idea the dog might go across to Boswell like that?" Tom asked.

"Abby did—when she said how it was necessary to reward an animal when he got something right. What really terrified me was that he might forget who had taught him that particular trick—and beg in front of Abby!"

Abby and Tom laughed, and they all looked down at Teddy, who was now fast asleep.

"It's apt, isn't it," Abby said, "that in the end he should play so important a part in nailing the man who planned his master's death?"

"You going to miss him, Abby?" Jessica asked.

"Of course I am. But I think he's a man's dog, really, and I know he'll have a fine home with Tom."

"I've only got temporary custody so far," Tom reminded her.

Jessica said, "Oh, I'm sure it'll be confirmed when the courts appoint a new executor, or whatever the procedure is."

"Hope so. First millionaire I've ever had to look after. But I promise you this. There's not going to be any special treatment. With me he'll have a real dog's life—in the best sense of the term."

"I wonder what's going to happen to the estate generally," Abby said.

He shrugged. "Only the lawyers can say. If you ask me, the Langleys might have a good case if they claimed Boswell unduly influenced Denton in the making of that will."

"I don't think Spenser will be lodging any claim," Jessica said. "But if Morgana and Echo got a bit more out of the estate, I for one wouldn't begrudge it them."

Tom looked at Abby. "And you're off back home to Kent."

She nodded. "Yes, in a couple of weeks—with Silver King. I'm going to concentrate on making the next Olympics."

"You'll be missed here."

"Thanks. There's an awful lot I'll miss. I was very happy here. But I don't think I ever could be again, after all that's happened.

"And you're off home to Maine," he said to Jessica.

"That's right."

"Well, be sure and come back and see us again. Me and Teddy, I mean."

"I'll certainly try," she promised. "It's nice to know I've made two friends here, at least."

"One thing I've got to ask you before you leave," he said. "Jessica, how the heck do you think up your plots?"

Epilogue

"WELL," Ethan Cragg asked, "did you have a good time?"

Jessica considered. "In some ways."

He raised his eyebrows. "You don't seem very sure. Weren't the lectures a success?"

"They were very well received, as a matter of fact."

"What about the horseback-riding?"

"I managed to stay on."

"And those were the two things you were worried about. I told you you'd be fine."

"You did, Ethan, and you were quite right."

"I suppose, knowing you, you'll be starting a new book right away?"

"No."

"Oh? Why's that?"

"Because frankly, what I want most of all after my vacation is a good long rest."

MURDER, SHE WROTE

Now a CBS-TV mystery series
starring Angela Lansbury as Jessica Fletcher,
a mystery writer turned detective

#1: The Murder of Sherlock Holmes
by James Anderson
89702-4/$2.95 US/$3.75 Can

#2: Hooray for Homicide
by James Anderson
89937-X/$2.95 US/$3.75 Can

#3: Lovers and Other Killers
by James Anderson
89938-8/$2.95 US/$3.75 Can

Also by James Anderson

The Affair of the Blood-Stained Egg Cosy
01919-1/$2.95 US/$3.75 Can

A classic 1930's whodunit right up until the moment the
suspects (and that's nearly everyone) assemble in the
drawing room.

The Affair of the Mutilated Mink Coat
78964-7/$2.95 US/$3.75 Can

A star-struck English Lord, a Hollywood producer, a
hot-tempered femme fatale, a butler named Merryweather
and a whole cast of zany characters in a particularly
pleasing puzzler of mistaken identity, a mutilated
mink coat...and murder.